Under Boy Scout Colors

By

Joseph Bushnell Ames

UNDER BOY SCOUT COLORS

CHAPTER I
THE LIVE WIRE

Dale Tompkins slung the bulging bag of papers over one shoulder, and, turning away from the news-stand, walked briskly down the main street of Hillsgrove. The rain had ceased, and the wind that had howled fiercely all day long was shifting into the west, where it tore to tatters the banks of dun gray clouds, letting through gleams and patches of cold blue sky tinged with the pale, chill yellow of a typical autumn sunset.

The cold look of that sunset was well borne out by a keen nip in the air, but Dale was too thankful to have it clear at all to complain. Besides, he wasn't exactly the complaining sort. Turning up the collar of a rather shabby coat, he thrust both hands deep into his trousers' pockets and hurried whistling along, bent on delivering his papers in the quickest possible time.

"I ought to get home by seven, anyhow," he thought calculatingly. "And if Mother'll only give me a hurry-up snack, I'll be in time for meeting."

He rolled the last word under his tongue with the prideful accent of a novice. Then, with a sudden start, one hand jerked out of his pocket and slipped between the buttons of the thread-bare coat. For an anxious moment it groped there before the fingers closed over a metal badge, shaped like a trefoil, that was pinned securely to the flannel shirt. A somewhat sheepish grin overspread the freckled face, and through an open gate Dale shot a paper dexterously across the porch to land accurately in the middle of the door-mat.

"I'd hate to lose it the very first week," he muttered, with a touch of apology. Mechanically he delivered another paper, and then he sighed. "Gee! A month sure seems an awful long time to wait when you know about all the tests already. I could even pass some of the first-class ones, I bet! That handbook's a dandy, all right. I don't guess there was ever another book printed with so much in it, exceptin', maybe–"

The words froze on his lips, and he caught his breath with a sharp, hissing intake. From somewhere in the next block a scream rang out on the still air, so shrill, so sudden, so full of surprise and pain and utter terror that Dale's blood turned cold within him, and the arm, half extended to toss a folded paper, halted in the middle of its swing, as if encountering an invisible obstacle. The pause was only momentary. Abruptly, as if two hands were pressed around a throbbing throat, the cry was cut off, and in the deathly silence that followed, Dale hurled the paper hastily, but accurately, from him, and turned and ran.

Eyes wide and face a little white, he tore across the road, splashing through puddles and slipping in the soft mud. Whirling around the corner into Pine Street, he saw a woman rush bareheaded out of a near-by house and two men come running down an adjacent alley. Rather, he noted them with that odd sense of observation which works intuitively, for his whole being was concentrated on the sight of that slight, boyish figure lying motionless in the roadway.

For a second Dale stared blankly, unable to understand. His first thought was that some human agency had done this thing, but almost as swiftly he realized that there was no one in sight who could have struck the child unconscious, nor had there been time for such an assailant to get away. Then, as he hurried closer through the gathering dusk, he caught sight of a trailing wire gripped convulsively in the small hands, and in a flash he realized the truth. In a flash, too, he realized that the body was not as motionless as he had supposed. A writhing, twisting movement, slight but ceaseless, quivered through the helpless victim, from his thin, black-stockinged legs to the blue lips. To the white-faced lad bending over him it seemed to tell of great suffering borne, perforce, in silence–and he was such a little kid!

From Dale's own lips there burst a smothered, inarticulate cry. Every idea, save the vital need of tearing loose that killing grip, vanished from the older boy's mind. Heedless of a warning shout from one of the men, he bent swiftly forward and caught the child by one shoulder.

What happened then Dale was never afterward able to describe clearly. It was as if some monstrous tingling force, greater, stranger than anything he had ever known, struck at him out of the air. In a twinkling it tore him from the boy on the ground and hurled him almost the width of the street. He crashed against the stone curbing and for a second or two lay there, dazed and blinking, then climbed painfully to his feet.

"I oughtn't to have–touched him–with my bare hands," he muttered uncertainly. "I must have got nearly the whole charge!"

He felt faint and sick and wobbly. From the horrified group gathered helplessly around the unconscious boy across the street, a woman's hysterical cry beat on his brain with monotonous iteration: "What can we do? What can we do? It's terrible! Oh, can't you do something?"

"If we only had rubber gloves–" murmured one of the men, vaguely.

"Where's a 'phone?" interrupted another. "I'm going to get 'em to shut off the current!"

"You can't," some one replied. People were constantly rushing up to gasp and exclaim, but do nothing. "The power-house is clear over at Medina. It'll take too long to get the connection."

"I'm going to try, anyhow," was the sharp retort. "It's better than doing nothing."

As he dashed past Dale and disappeared into a neighboring house, the boy moved slowly forward. He splashed through a puddle, and something he had read, or heard, came back to him. Water was a perfect conductor, and he had been standing in a regular pool of it when he grabbed the child. No wonder he had been shocked.

"Insulation," he murmured, his head still swimming. "That's it! The handbook says–"

The bag of papers bumped against his thigh, and somehow Dale's numbed brain began to clear swiftly. How could he have forgotten that paper was a non-conductor as well as silk or rubber? Rubber! Why, the bag itself was made of some kind of waterproof stuff. He thrust aside a half-grown, gaping youth.

"Give me a show, can't you?" he cried almost fiercely. Thrilled, exhilarated with a sudden sense of power, he jerked the bag off his shoulder. "The kid'll never live if he waits for you fellows to do something." With extraordinary swiftness he pulled out several thicknesses of newspaper and wrapped them about one hand and arm. Similarly swathing the other, he dropped the rubber-coated bag to the ground and stepped squarely on it. His eyes were wide and almost black with excitement. "Oh, cut that out!" he snapped over one shoulder to a protesting bystander. "Don't you s'pose I know what I'm doing? I'm a scout!"

A second later he had gripped the unconscious child again by an arm and shoulder. This time there was no shock, only a queer, vibratory tingling that

Dale scarcely noticed, so intent was he on doing the right thing. He must not bungle now. He remembered perfectly what the book said about releasing a person in contact with a live wire. It must be done quickly and cleanly, without unnecessary tugging, or else the shock and burning would be greatly increased. Dale braced his feet and drew a long breath. Then, suddenly, he jerked backward with all the strength he could summon. The next thing he knew he was sitting squarely in a puddle with both arms around the child, whose grip on the deadly wire he had broken.

Instantly the hitherto inactive group was roused to life and movement, and amidst a Babel of talk and advice they surged around the unconscious lad and his rescuer. Before the latter realized what had happened, some one had snatched the little chap from him and started swiftly toward one of the near-by houses. After and around them streamed a throng of men, women, and children, pitying, anxious, or merely curious, but, now that the danger was past, all equally voluble with suggestions or advice.

Dale rose slowly to his feet, and stood for a moment staring after them with a troubled frown. "Why don't they give him air?" he said. "If only they wouldn't bunch around him like that–"

He paused hesitatingly, watching the procession mount the steps and cross a wide veranda. The stress and excitement that had dominated him till now seemed to have vanished, and a reaction set in. He wondered whether folks wouldn't think him too "fresh" for thrusting himself forward as he had done. The remembrance of the man to whom he had talked back made him wriggle uncomfortably; it was one of his oldest customers. "Gee!" he muttered, with a touch of uneasiness; "I reckon I must have sassed him pretty well, too!"

Dusk had given place to night. Under a flaring gas-light at the curb two early arrivals, who had stayed behind to guard the deadly, dangling wire, were busy explaining the situation to several wide-eyed later comers. They formed an animated group, and Dale, standing in the shadow behind them, felt curiously out of it and alone. The wind, sweeping up the street, struck through his wet clothes and made him shiver.

"Time I was getting started," he thought. "It must be awful late."

As he bent over to pick up his bag, the movement set his head to throbbing afresh. His exploring fingers encountered a lump, where he had hit the curb, that felt about the size of an ostrich-egg. Dale's forehead wrinkled, and he opened the bag mechanically, only to find the remaining papers were soaked through and ruined. Those he had wrapped around his hands lay in the mud at his feet, soggy masses of pulp. And he had delivered only four out of the lot!

Dale tried to smile, but his lips only quivered. With a second, more determined, effort, he clenched his teeth tightly, slung the empty bag over his shoulder, and started back toward the news-stand. But he went in silence. Somehow the usual whistle was impossible.

CHAPTER II

THE NEW TENDERFOOT

It was close to half past seven before Dale delivered his last paper. He had been delayed in the beginning by old Jed Hathaway's having to know all about it, and insisting on hearing every little detail before he could be induced to provide a second supply. Dale tried to be patient under the cross-examination of the garrulous old newsdealer, but it wasn't easy when he knew that each minute wasted now was going to make it harder to get through in time for the scout meeting. When he was released at last, he hurried all he could, but the minute-hand of the old town-clock was perilously close to the perpendicular when he got back to the square again.

Clearly, there was no time to go home even for that "hurry up" snack he had been thinking about. There wasn't even time to get a sandwich from the lunch-wagon, two blocks away. "Have to pull in my belt and forget about it till I get home after meeting, I reckon," he thought.

In suiting the action to the word he realized that his hurried efforts at the news-stand to clean off the mud had been far from successful. It plastered his person, if not from head to foot, at least from the waist down, and now that it was beginning to dry, it seemed to show up more distinctly each moment. He couldn't present himself before Scoutmaster Curtis in such a plight, so he raced across the square to his friend Joe Banta's shoe-cleaning establishment, borrowed a stiff brush, and went to work vigorously.

Brief as was the delay, it sufficed to make him late. Though not at all sectarian, Troop Five held its weekly meetings in the parish-house of the Episcopal church, whose rector was intensely interested in the movement. These were scheduled for seven-thirty on Monday evenings. There was usually a brief delay for belated scouts, but by twenty minutes of eight, at latest, the shrill blast of the scoutmaster's whistle brought the fellows at attention, ready for the salute to the flag and the other simple exercises that opened the meeting.

Precisely one minute later Dale Tompkins burst hastily into the vestibule and pulled up abruptly. Through the open door a long line of khaki-clad backs confronted him, trim, erect, efficient-looking. Each figure stood rigidly at attention, shoulders back, eyes set straight ahead, three fingers pressed against the forehead in the scout salute, and lips moving in unison over the last words of the scout oath.

"... To keep myself physically strong, mentally awake, and morally straight."

"Colors post!" came crisply from the scoutmaster facing the line.

From the shadows of the entry Dale felt a sort of thrill at the precision of the movement and the neatness with which the slim color-bearer, who had faced the line just in front of Mr. Curtis and his assistant, pivoted on his heel and bore the flag, its silken folds gently rippling, past the scouts still standing at attention and on out of sight toward the farther end of the room.

Of course it was only Courtlandt Parker, who was in Dale's grade at school and a very familiar person indeed. But somehow, in this rôle, he did not seem nearly so familiar and intimate. To the watching tenderfoot it was almost as if he had ceased for the moment to be the airy, volatile, harum-scarum "Court," whose pranks and witticisms so often kept the whole grade stirred up and amused, and had become solely the sober, earnest, serious color-bearer of the troop.

"A lot of it's the uniform, of course," thought Dale. "It does make a whopping difference in a fellow's looks." He glanced down at his own worn, still disheveled garments with sudden distaste. "I wish I had mine!" he sighed.

A moment later, still hesitating in the background, reluctant to face that trim, immaculate line, he caught the scoutmaster's glance,–that level, friendly, smiling glance, which was at once a salutation and a welcome,–and his head went up abruptly. What did looks matter, after all–at least the sort of looks one couldn't help? He was none the worse a scout because he had not yet saved up enough money for that coveted suit of khaki. Nor was it his fault that he had lacked the time to go home and brush up thoroughly for the meeting. He smiled back a little at Mr. Curtis, and then, with shoulders square and head erect, he obeyed the leader's silent summons.

There was a faint stir and a sense of curious, shifting eyes when he appeared around the end of the line of waiting scouts. As he passed Sherman Ward's patrol some one even whispered an airy greeting, "Aye, Tommy." Though Dale did not glance that way, he knew it to be the irrepressible Courtlandt, now returned to his position as assistant patrol-leader. Court was the only one who ever called him that, and the boy's heart warmed at this touch of friendliness.

Then he paused before the scoutmaster and promptly, though perhaps a little awkwardly, returned the man's salute.

"I'm glad to see you, Dale," the scoutmaster said, in a tone which robbed the words of any trace of the perfunctory. "I'd begun to think something was keeping you away to-night."

The boy flushed a little. "I–I was delayed, sir," he explained briefly. "I–I–it won't happen again, sir."

"Good!" The scoutmaster nodded approval, his glance sweeping meditatively over the three patrols. He was slim and dark, with eyes set wide apart, and a humorous, rather sensitive mouth. The boys liked him without exactly knowing why, for he was not the popular athletic type of scoutmaster, nor yet the sort of man who dominates by sheer force of personality and commands immense respect if nothing more.

"Most of you fellows know Dale Tompkins, our new tenderfoot," he went on presently, raising his voice a little. "For the benefit of those who don't, I'll say that he passed an extra good examination last week, and I've an idea he's going to be a credit to the troop. He will take Arnold's place in Wolf patrol, which brings us up to our full strength again. That's the one at the head of the line, Tompkins. Patrol-leader Ranleigh Phelps will take you in charge and show you the ropes."

Dale's heart leaped, and a sudden warm glow came over him. He had never exchanged a word with Ranny Phelps, and yet the handsome, dashing leader of Wolf patrol probably had more to do with Tompkins' becoming a member of Troop Five than any other cause. The boy liked Mr. Curtis, to be sure, and was glad to have him for a scoutmaster, but his feeling for Phelps, though he had never expressed it even to himself, was something deeper than mere liking. To him, the good-looking, blond chap seemed everything that a scout should be and so seldom was. Perhaps one of the reasons was because he always contrived to look the part so satisfyingly. Whenever the troop appeared in public, Phelps's uniform fitted to perfection, his bearing was invariably beyond criticism, his execution of the various manœuvers was crisp, snappy, faultless. In athletic events, too, he was always prominent, entering in almost every event, and coming out ahead in many. And he was physically so picturesque with his clean-cut features, gray eyes, and mass of curly blond hair, his poise and perfect self-possession, that gradually in the breast of the rugged, unornamental Tompkins there had grown up a shy admiration, a silent, wistful liking which strengthened as time went on almost to hero-worship, yet which, of course, he would have perished sooner than reveal. When he had at length gained his father's grudging permission to become a scout, it was this feeling mainly which prompted him to make application to Troop Five. He had not dared to hope that Mr. Curtis would actually assign him to Ranny Phelps's patrol.

"You mean I–I'm to stay in–in Wolf patrol, sir?" he stammered incredulously.

The scoutmaster nodded. "It's the only vacancy. Both the others are filled. Ranny will show you where your place is, and then we'll proceed with the drill."

With face a little flushed, the tenderfoot turned and took a few steps toward the head of the line. Just what he expected from his hero he could not have said. Perhaps he vaguely felt that Phelps would step forward and shake his hand, or at least greet the new-comer with a welcoming smile. But Ranny did not stir from his place. Stiff and straight he stood there, and as Tompkins paused hesitatingly, the shapely lips curled unpleasantly at the corners, and the gray eyes ranged slowly over him from head to heel and back again in a manner that sent the blood surging into the boy's face and brought his lids down abruptly to hide the swift surprise and hurt that flashed into his brown eyes.

"At the end of the line, tenderfoot," ordered Phelps, curtly. "And don't be all day about it!"

The latter words were in an undertone which could not well have reached beyond the ears of the lad for whom they were intended. The chill unfriendliness of the whole remark affected Dale Tompkins much like a douche of ice-cold water. With head suddenly erect and lips compressed, he swiftly took his place at the end of the patrol, next to a plump, red-cheeked boy named Vedder, who, save for a brief, swiftly averted side-glance, gave no further evidence of welcome than had the leader.

In the brief pause that followed while the assistant patrol-leaders procured staves and distributed them, the tenderfoot tried to solve the problem. What was the matter? he asked himself in troubled bewilderment. What had he done that was wrong? Naturally a cheerful, friendly soul, he could not imagine himself, were their positions reversed, treating a stranger with such chill formality. But perhaps he had expected too much. After all, there was no reason why the fellows should break ranks in the middle of meeting and fall on his neck, when not more than a third of the crowd had ever spoken to him before. For a moment he had forgotten that while he had long ardently admired Ranny Phelps from afar, the blond chap had probably never even heard his name before. It would be different when they came to know each other.

Cheered by this thought, Dale braced up and flung himself with characteristic ardor into acquiring the various movements of the drill. These were not difficult, but somehow, try as he might, he could not seem to satisfy his leader. At every slightest error, or even hesitation, Ranny flew out at him with a caustic sharpness that swiftly got the tenderfoot's nerve and made him blunder more than ever. Yet still he found excuses for the fellow he so admired.

"You can't blame anybody for not liking to coach up a greenhorn when all the rest of them do it so well," he said to himself after the meeting was over and the boys were leaving the hall. "It's the best patrol of the three, all right, and I'll just have to get busy and learn the drill, so's not to make a single mistake." He sighed a little. "I wish–"

"What's the matter, Dale? Seems to me you're looking mighty serious."

A hand dropped on his shoulder, and Dale glanced swiftly up to meet the quizzical, inquiring gaze of Mr. Curtis. He hesitated an instant, a touch of embarrassment in his answering smile.

"Nothing much, sir," he returned. "I was just thinking what a dub I am at that drill, and wishing–a complete uniform costs six-thirty, doesn't it, Mr. Curtis?"

The scoutmaster nodded. "Would you like me to order one for you?"

Dale laughed a little wistfully. "I sure would!" he ejaculated fervently. "The trouble is I only have about four dollars and that isn't enough."

"Not quite," The man hesitated an instant, his eyes on the boy's face. "I'll tell you what we can do, though," he went on slowly. "If you like, I'll advance the difference so that you can have it right away, and you can pay me back whenever it's convenient."

For a moment Dale did not speak. Then he shook his head regretfully. "It's mighty good of you, sir, but I guess I'd better–" He paused abruptly, and a slow flush crept into his face. "Does a fellow have to have one? Would I be–that is, if I didn't have one for a while, will it–make a lot of difference for the other fellows–will it look bad for the troop?"

Mr. Curtis laughed suddenly, and his hand tightened a bit on the boy's shoulder. "Bless you, no!" he exclaimed. "Get rid of that notion right away. I thoroughly believe in every scout's wanting a uniform, and working for it, and wearing it whenever he can, and being proud of it, but I'd hate awfully to have him feel that he was out of place in Troop Five without one. It's the spirit that makes the scout, not clothes, and I'm just a little glad you didn't accept my offer, Dale. Keep on saving for it, and, when you've enough, come to me. Meanwhile–you say you didn't get the drill very well?"

"No, sir. I was rank."

"That's because you're new to it, and to the crowd, and everything. It really isn't hard. If you can come around to my house after supper to-morrow night, I'll coach you up in half an hour so you can't make a mistake next Friday if you try. That'll put you on even terms with the rest of the troop, and make you forget this little matter of clothes. How about it?"

Dale's eyes brightened. "That would be corking, sir! Of course I can come, only won't it be a trouble to you?"

"Not a bit. Come any time after seven. You know where I live, don't you?"

"Yes, sir. I'll be there, all right; and thank you ever so much for helping me."

"You needn't," smiled the scoutmaster. "It will be a pleasure." He dropped his hand and was turning away when his glance rested on the boy's solid-looking shoulders and then traveled on down over the lithe frame. "Play football?" he asked, with a touch of fresh interest.

Dale nodded eagerly. "Yes, sir; as much as I've had time for, that is. Do–do you think I'd have any show for the team?"

"I shouldn't wonder. See Sherman Ward; he's captain. The season's half over, but we need weight behind the line, and it wouldn't surprise me if you'd do. Try it, anyhow. Good night; see you to-morrow."

Dale found his cap and slipped out of the building, a pleasant glow stealing over him. "He's corking!" he muttered, as he followed the flagged walk that led past the shadowy bulk of the stone church to the street. "He makes a fellow feel–well, sort of as if he belonged!"

He had been a chump to let himself be troubled by Ranny Phelps's brusqueness. "Of course he was peeved when I made such a mess of things," he thought. "Just wait till next Friday, though, and he'll–"

Dale's progress along the walk and his train of thought stopped abruptly at one and the same time. He had reached the side of the squat stone tower that faced the street, but was still in the shadow, when the voice of Ranny Phelps, somewhat shrill with temper and unmistakably scornful of accent, smote suddenly on his ears.

"The idea of a mucker like that being in Troop Five–and in my own patrol, too! It's simply sickening! You saw him to-night; so stupid he couldn't even learn the drill, and did anybody ever see such clothes? They look as if they'd come out of the rag-bag."

An indistinguishable murmur in another voice seemed merely to goad the irate patrol-leader to increased frenzy.

"That's just it–a common newsboy! He'll be an ornament to the troop, won't he? He'll make a fine-looking scout, he will! I can just see what a rotten mess he'll make of the line if we should have to march in public. Mr. Curtis must be crazy to take in such riffraff, and I've half a mind to tell him–"

The rest of the remark was indistinguishable, for the speakers were moving away from the church in the direction of the better class, residential section. Presently, even the rising and falling murmur of voices ceased, but still the figure in the shadow of the church tower did not stir. When at last he moved slowly forward into the circle of an electric light, something of the hard grayness of the stone might almost have come into his face.

"'A scout is a friend to all and a brother to every other scout,'" he said, half aloud, as he turned in an opposite direction to that taken by Phelps and his companion.

Then he laughed. It wasn't exactly a pleasant sound. There was no mirth in it; only scorn, derision, and, under all the rest, a note of pain that could not quite be hidden.

CHAPTER III

THE SILVER LINING

"Say, fellows, did you hear about Jimmy Warren's kid brother?" eagerly inquired Court Parker, skipping up to a group gathered about the school steps next morning.

From force of habit, expectant grins wreathed several faces. "Huh!" grunted Bob Gibson, suspiciously. "What's the joke?"

"Joke!" repeated the latest comer, indignantly. "There isn't any joke. What gave you that idea? It came pretty near being serious, I can tell you. One of the electric feed-wires got loose in the storm yesterday, and hung down in front of Jimmy's house on Pine Street. Before anybody else saw it, that crazy kid Georgie had to go out and grab hold of it with both hands."

He paused an instant for breath, and a concerted exclamation went up from the crowd that had gathered swiftly about him. "Gee!" exclaimed stout Harry Vedder. "And the current still on, I s'pose?"

"Of course it was! Dad told me how many volts. I forget. Anyhow, Georgie got hold and couldn't let go. They said he yelled to beat the band, and then went clean out. A crowd got around right away, but nobody seemed to know what to do. One man ran in and started 'phoning for 'em to turn off the current; and while he was gone, what do you think happened? A kid with a bunch of papers came along, and jumped right in and grabbed hold of Georgie to pull him off the wire. They said that when the current hit him it was like being kicked by a horse. He went clean across the street and banged his head an awful whack on the curb. He got up sort of groggy, but he must have been a game one, for he came right back, wrapped some newspapers around his hands, and had Georgie loose in a jiffy!"

"Great!" came in an appreciative chorus. Then one of the third-grade boys piped up curiously. "But what good was the newspaper?"

"Insulation, of course," spoke up Sherman Ward, from the outskirts of the group. He was tall enough to look over the heads of most of the fellows, and spoke with a certain authority. "If he hadn't used them he'd have got the shock as he did the first time. That's some idea, though, fellows. I don't believe I'd have remembered, right off the bat, that paper was a non-conductor. Who was he, Court?"

"Nobody knows; that's the funny part of it." Court thrust back a dangling lock of brown hair with a characteristic gesture. "It was pretty near dark, and everybody was excited, and all that, Mrs. Warren told Dad when he was over this morning. She said she only noticed that he wasn't so very tall and carried his papers in a bag over one shoulder. She forgot all about him till after they'd got the kid into the house and the doctor had come. Then when she sent somebody out to see, the chap had gone."

At once the throng of boys was plunged into a fever of interested speculation. The idea of an unknown appearing suddenly out of the darkness, doing his spectacular stunt, and slipping away again without revealing himself appealed tremendously to the imagination. The fact that he was a boy and quite possibly one of themselves vastly increased the interest. One after another the various fellows with paper routes were suggested, but for the most part as quickly dismissed. One was too tall, another delivered in a different part of town, two more were part of the present assemblage and reluctantly denied any connection with the affair.

"Maybe it was that fellow Tompkins," doubtfully suggested Bob Gibson, when most of the other possibilities had been exhausted. "He goes past Pine Street, doesn't he?"

A sudden low laugh touched with scorn, from the outskirts of the circle, turned all eyes to where Ranny Phelps leaned against the iron railing.

"You're quite a joker, aren't you, Bob?" commented the blond chap, with a flash of his white teeth.

Gibson sniffed. "I don't see anything so awful funny in that," he retorted. "He does go past Pine Street about every night; I've seen him often."

"Quite possibly," agreed Phelps, suavely. "I never said he didn't, you old grumbler. He probably went past last night, but take my word for it he didn't turn in. You don't suppose that thickhead would have the gumption to do what this chap did, or the wit to know about paper being a non-conductor, and all that? Not in a thousand years!"

Bob's mouth set stubbornly; he was one who never lost a chance to argue. "I don't see it at all!" he retorted. "Just because you say so doesn't make him thick. I noticed you picking on him last night, and I tell you right now that anybody might seem–"

"He didn't seem brainless–he was," interrupted Phelps with cool, scornful certainty. "A fellow who could manage to fall over his feet as many times as he did in that simple little drill, and make as many breaks–"

He paused suddenly and bit his lips. At the farther edge of the wide circle the face of Tompkins himself had loomed all at once into his surprised consciousness, and something in the boy's level, unsmiling, somber glance brought a twinge of shame to Ranleigh's heart. For an instant he stood silent, striving to resume his usual cool nonchalance. Then he turned away with a shrug.

"But after all," he drawled, "it's hardly worth while arguing about. Who's got that seventh problem in Geom? It's a sticker, all right."

It was well enough done to deceive most of the fellows about him, particularly since the sound of the last bell started the crowd up the steps and into the school building. But Court Parker had noted the direction of Ranny's glance, and a gleam of indignation flashed into his eyes. For a moment he stood biting his lips; then his face cleared and he pounced on Tompkins.

"Well, were you, Tommy!" he demanded airily.

"Was I what?" countered the other, briefly.

"The hero–the chap who leaped into the breach and saved Georgie Warren from a–a–an electrocutive finish." Court's metaphors might be mixed, but his vocabulary seldom lacked originality. Tompkins merely shrugged his shoulders and frowned a bit.

"Is it likely?" he asked, with a touch of bitterness. "Even if I'd had the chance, I'm too thick to–"

"Rot!" cut in Court, swiftly. As they went up the steps he flung an arm impulsively around the other's shoulders. "Don't you worry about anything Ranny Phelps says. Nobody ever pays any attention to him, anyhow. I do wish I knew who that plucky chap was, though. It was a corking thing to do. You haven't heard any one say, have you, Tommy?"

Tompkins hesitated an instant, an odd indecision in his face. A few minutes ago he might have found a boyish pride and pleasure in his friend's surprise at learning his part in the affair. Now he merely shook his head. "Those I've heard–talking about it, didn't seem to know," he returned shortly.

"Humph! Well, I guess I'll have to start my mighty brain working and do the Sherlock Holmes stunt," decided Court, philosophically. "Say! Won't Jimmy be crazy, though, to be away at school with all this happening to his own family. I can just see him squirm!"

As they entered the coat-room his volatile mind leaped to another topic. "There's one good thing, old top; you can come out for the troop team now. That'll be great! Don't forget there's practice right after school this aft."

Dale slapped his cap on a hook and turned away. "I'm not coming out," he said gruffly, making for the door.

Court's eyes widened. "Not coming out for football!" he repeated amazedly.

"No!"

"Why not, for goodness' sake?"

"I don't want to," was the almost ungracious retort.

Court sniffed incredulously. "Tell that to your grandmother! Haven't I seen you play often enough to know better? Wait a second." At the entrance of the coat-room he caught Tompkins by the arm, and, whirling him around, stared into his face. "If you think for a minute," he went on with some heat, "that anybody– You old idiot! You make me sick with your silly notions. I'll–I'll settle you, though."

With which cryptic and somewhat fragmentary comment, he slapped Dale briskly on the back and slipped into his seat, leaving the other to seek his own place on the farther side of the room, unconsciously heartened a bit by his fellow's friendliness. But a moment later his forehead wrinkled perplexedly. Court had a little habit of impulsively settling the affairs of nations offhand, and his last remark seemed to indicate that something of the kind was in his mind at present.

"Well, whatever it is, he won't get me to come out for the team," decided Tompkins, his jaw squaring stubbornly. "They don't think I'm good enough for them, and I'm not going to force myself where I'm not wanted."

Those few words overheard just before had opened afresh the wound of the night before and confirmed Dale's conviction that he was not wanted in Troop Five. With the exception of one or two of the boys who had been friendly before, he felt that the scouts agreed with Ranny Phelps in resenting his presence in the crack troop of Hillsgrove. Because his father was a working-man, because he himself sold papers to eke out the family income, because, in short, he was poor and had come to meeting in rather shabby clothes instead of a natty uniform, they looked down on him as an interloper who had no business to be there. He would merely be inviting further slights by appearing on the football field and trying for a position on the troop eleven.

"I can just see Sherman Ward's expression if I did!" he thought bitterly. "He's the niftiest one of the lot, with his father owning the iron works and about half the town besides. He wouldn't waste much time on me, I guess!"

Taken all in all, Dale failed to pass either a pleasant or a profitable morning. He tried to keep his mind on the lessons, but that wasn't easy. He had not yet decided whether or not to remain in the troop, and this question seemed so much more vital and important than arithmetic problems or dates in ancient history that his thoughts returned to it again and again. He hated the idea of staying where he wasn't wanted, and yet to leave now would look as if he were a coward, afraid to face the jibes and sarcasms of the fellows who didn't like him.

The end of the morning session found the problem still unsolved. Dale was a little slow putting his books away, and when he came to look for Parker, who usually walked home with him, Court was nowhere to be seen. As he left the building he noticed a bunch of high-school boys from upstairs laughing and fooling on the corner. Ranny Phelps was among them, and several other members of Troop Five, and unconsciously the tenderfoot paused for an instant and half turned as if to seek the other exit. A second later his lips tightened and a dull flush came into his cheeks. He never went home that way, why should he take it now? Swiftly he turned back, and with head high in a desperate effort to look unconscious, he started briskly down the walk. He was within a dozen feet of the jolly group when all at once there came a hail from behind.

"Hi, Dale!"

Astonished, he turned at the call to see Sherman Ward coming down the school steps. For a moment it seemed as if he must have been mistaken, but the older chap quickly settled that doubt.

"Wait a minute, kid," he went on; "I want to talk to you."

In an instant Dale's interest in the throng at the corner vanished. Surprised, curious, a little on the defensive, he watched the approach of the senior patrol-leader.

"I forgot to speak to you last night about football," Sherman began at once with brisk, casual friendliness. "You play, don't you?"

"A–a little," stammered Dale, dazed by the absence of what he had so fully expected in the other's manner.

"What position?"

"Er–tackle, and–and half-back–sometimes."

"You ought to be a pretty good back if you've got speed," mused the older chap, his glance appreciatively taking in the boy's sturdy build and good shoulders. "The season's well along and the team's made up, but we need more weight. Troop One's the only team we're afraid of, but we've simply got to lick them and nab the pennant. I'll try you out this afternoon. Practice at three-thirty sharp in the field back of my place. We'll go right over from school. You go this way, don't you?"

The throng at the corner had broken up, and the two were practically alone. Dale nodded and mechanically fell into step. He had been steeling himself for something so very different that in a second his defenses were swept entirely away. Ward's perfect assurance of his readiness to play made even hesitation seem the action of a selfish cad unwilling to do his best for his troop. Besides, Dale did not want to refuse–now.

"How is it you never thought of being a scout before?" asked Ward, as they cut across corners toward Main Street. "Wasn't there any troop where you came from?"

Dale shook his head. "No; and after we got here Father–didn't want me to join. He–he didn't seem to understand about it, and so–"

He paused; Ward nodded comprehendingly. "Sometimes they don't," he said. "Well, it's all right now. You're in, and you don't look like a chap who'd stay a tenderfoot long, especially with a scoutmaster like Mr. Curtis. He's a corker, all right, and does everything to help a fellow along. I shouldn't wonder if you'd be ready for second-class exams as soon as the month is up."

Dale's eyes brightened. "I'll certainly try 'em, anyhow. I can pass a lot of the tests now, I think, and I'm going to bone up on the others hard."

"That's the boy!" smiled Sherman. "If I can help you in anything, let me know. Well, this is my corner. So long. Don't forget practice at three-thirty sharp."

With a wave of his hand he turned down Main Street, leaving Dale to stare after him for a moment or two, an odd expression on his freckled face.

"Why, he's–he's not a bit what I– He's just like–" He ended with a deep-drawn breath and turned homeward, head high and shoulders squared.

Somehow the blue of the sky seemed suddenly deeper, the sunshine brighter than it had been before. The crisp, clean autumn air had a tang in it he had not noticed until this moment. He drew it into his lungs in great gulps, and his eyes sparkled.

"The pants'll do," he murmured to himself; "so will the jersey. I haven't any decent shoes, but I've played in sneakers before. And there'll be time to deliver the papers after five."

CHAPTER IV

ON THE GRIDIRON

Ranny Phelps left the school building that afternoon in a distinctly disagreeable mood. He had been feeling vaguely irritable all day, but since noon there had developed grouchy tendencies, as Court Parker termed them, and he was ready to flare up at the slightest provocation. On the way down-stairs he had flown out at Harry Vedder, one of his particular followers, for no other reason than that the stout youth expressed an indolent conviction that the new tenderfoot could play football better than he could drill, and that he would probably show up on the field. The blow-up, instead of relieving pressure, as such things often do, seemed to deepen Phelps's discontent, and seeing Ward on the walk just ahead of him, he yielded to a sudden impulse and hastily caught up with him.

"Look here, Sherm," he began hastily, "you're not really thinking of–of–using that nut Tompkins, are you?"

The football captain glanced sidewise at him–a cool, level stare. "Why not?" he asked briefly. "He's a member of the troop, isn't he?"

Ranny realized his mistake, but temper kept him to it. "Oh, yes! yes, of course," he snapped petulantly. "Unfortunately he is, but I don't see why you should encourage him. If he's shown that he–he–isn't wanted, he may have the wit to–to–"

Conscious of Ward's prolonged, quizzical glance, the blond chap faltered, and then, furious at himself and with his companion, he went on angrily: "You needn't look like that. You know yourself he's the extreme limit. Look at him now!" He waved one hand jerkily toward a group ahead, which included the boy under discussion chatting eagerly with Parker and Bob Gibson. "He's a disgrace to the troop with that horrible-looking suit, all rags and frayed, and–and his hair brushing all over his collar; I don't believe it's been cut in months."

"Well, what of it?" inquired the taller chap composedly, as Ranny paused for breath. "What's his hair or his clothes got to do with his being a good scout?"

"Everything!" snapped Ranny, biting his lips and striving to keep down his temper. "A fellow that amounts to anything will–will keep himself decent looking even if he is–poor. Besides he–you saw him last night; couldn't do the simplest thing without making a show of himself. Take my word for it, he'll never amount to anything. He's a dead loss, and I wish– I can't think what you see in–"

He broke off with grating teeth, maddeningly conscious of the futility and ineffectiveness of his words. It wasn't at all the sort of thing he had meant to say. He realized that temper had deadened judgment, and that the whole must sound excessively silly and childish. He fully expected his companion to greet the outbreak with open ridicule, but when he looked up, he discovered with mingled annoyance and relief that Ward wasn't listening at all. Instead, he was staring at the group ahead with an expression of such frank curiosity and interest that instinctively Ranny followed the direction of his schoolmate's eager glance.

Eight or ten boys, mostly upper-grade grammar-school students and about half of them scouts, were bunched together at the corner of a cross-street. Apparently they had been halted by a man of middle age who was talking with considerable animation, the while keeping one hand on the shoulder of Dale Tompkins, who looked exceedingly sheepish and uncomfortable. As Ranny stared, puzzled, he was amazed to see Court Parker leap suddenly at his classmate with a piercing yell, clutch him about the waist, and execute a few steps of a wildly eccentric war-dance. Then he thumped the tenderfoot violently on the back, and finally the whole crowd flung themselves on the boy in a body. As Ward and Phelps hastily approached, the victim was engulfed by numbers, but his vehement, embarrassed protests sounded intermittently above the din.

"Aw, quit it, fellows! Lay off, won't you? It wasn't anything. I– Cut it out–do!"

"Here's the missing hero!" called Court Parker, shrilly. "Where's the leather medal?" Suddenly he slid out of the throng and faced the new-comers, his eyes shining. "What do you know about Tommy?" he demanded. "He's the mysterious guy who rescued Georgie Warren last night. Fact! Mr. Pegram was there and saw him. He was the one who 'phoned the company to shut off the current, you know. Says Tommy was cool as a cucumber and had all kinds of nerve And this morning he never let out a peep about it, even when I asked him. Some kid, eh, Sherm?"

Ward grinned. "The secretive young beggar!" he exclaimed. "By jinks! That ought to mean a medal, sure! And he a tenderfoot only a week!"

"Aw, quit it, fellows! It wasn't anything"

He moved forward toward the throng, eager for further details. Ranny did not stir. His face was blank, and his mind, usually so active, failed for a second or two to take in the meaning of what he had heard. When at length he realized the truth, a sense of grudging admiration stole over him. From one of those present at the affair last night he had had an unusually vivid account of the accident. He understood the risks the hitherto unknown rescuer had run, and fully appreciated his nerve and resourcefulness. For a flashing second he was filled with an impulse to follow Ward's example and add his brief word of congratulation to the chorus, but the impulse was only momentary. In a second or two he had crushed it back, passed the noisy group, and headed toward the football field alone.

How absurd he had been even to think of such a thing! The details had probably been greatly exaggerated. Doubtless, Tompkins had merely blundered into the affair and done the right thing through sheer fool luck. At any rate, he still remained precisely the same individual whose presence Ranny had considered a blot on the appearance of the troop and likely to injure its "tone." There seemed to him no reason why this latest development should alter his treatment of the fellow a particle.

Ward and the rest reached the field not long after Phelps, and no time was lost in commencing practice. Tompkins was started off with the scrub, an organization composed mostly of scouts who were too small or lazy or indifferent or unskilful to make the regular eleven, together with a few outsiders who had been persuaded into lending their aid merely for the fun of the game. It was a motley crowd, and Sherman had his hands full holding them together. One or two, to be sure, were stimulated by the hope, which grew fainter with each day of practice, that they might supplant some member of the regular team in time to play in the game of the season, the struggle with the redoubtable Troop One, which would end the series and decide the championship. But the majority had no such dominating incentive. Their interest flagged continually, and it was only by a constant appeal to their scout spirit, by rebuke and ridicule, interspersed with well-timed jollying, that they could be kept to the scratch. When Dale Tompkins was given the position of right tackle, the boy whose place he had taken openly rejoiced, and not a few of his companions viewed the escape with envy.

The regulars started with the ball, and the first down netted them eight yards. The second plunge through the line was almost as successful; the third even more so. The scrub played apathetically, each fellow for himself. They lacked cohesion, and many of the individuals opposed the rushes half-heartedly and without spirit. Little Saunders, the scrub quarter, while working at full pressure himself, seemed to have grown discouraged by past failures to spur the fellows on. Occasionally he snapped out a rasping appeal for them to get together and do something, but there was a perfunctory note in his voice which told how little faith he had in their obeying.

To Ward, playing at left half on the regulars, it was an old story which had ceased, almost, to fret him. He had come to feel that the utmost he could hope for was to keep the scrub together and gain what practice was possible from their half-hearted resistance. Keeping his eye on Tompkins, he noted with approval that the boy was playing a very different sort of game. He flung himself into the fray with snap and energy, tackling well, recovering swiftly, and showing a pretty knowledge of interference. But it was soon apparent that his work failed more or less because of its very quickness. At every rush he was a foot or two ahead of the sluggish Vedder at guard or the discouraged Morris playing on his right. He might get his man and frequently did, but one player cannot do all the work of a team, and the holes in the line remained as gaping as before.

The regulars scored a touchdown and, returning to the center of the field, began the process anew. There was a sort of monotonous iteration about their advance that presently began to get a little on Sherman's nerves. The crisp, shrill voice of Court Parker calling the signal, the thud of feet over the turf, the crash as the wedge of bodies struck the wavering line and thrust its way through it and on, on, seemingly to endless distance in spite of the plucky efforts of the boy at right tackle to stop it–it was all so cut and dried, so certain, so unvaried. Now and again would come the tired, ill-tempered snap of Saunders's "Get into it, fellows! Wake up, for the love of Pete!" Occasionally, from left end, Ranny Phelps would make some sarcastic reference to Ward's "great find," to which, though it irritated him, the captain paid no heed. He was still watching critically and beginning to wonder, with a little touch of anxiety, whether Tompkins was going to be engulfed in the general slough of inertia. In this wise the play had progressed half-way toward the scrub's goal-posts when suddenly a new note was injected into the affair.

"Steady, fellows. Let's get together. It's just as easy to fight back as to be walked over–and a lot more fun. Hold 'em, now!"

The voice was neither shrill nor snappish, but pitched in a sort of good-natured urgency. One guessed that the owner of it was growing weary of being eternally buffeted and flung aside. Ranny Phelps greeted the remark with a sarcastic laugh.

"Great head!" he jeered. "You must be quite an expert in the game. Why don't you try it?"

Dale Tompkins raised his head and dashed one hand across a dripping forehead. "That's what we're going to do," he smiled; "aren't we, Morris, old man? Come ahead, Vedder; all we need is a little team-work, fellows."

Stout Harry Vedder merely grunted breathlessly. But somehow, when the next rush came, his fat shoulders dropped a little lower and he lunged forward a shade more swiftly than he had done. Wilks, the weakest point in the opposing line, caught unexpectedly by the elephantine rush, went down, and Tompkins brought the man with the ball to earth by a nice tackle.

"That's the stuff," he gasped as he scrambled up. "Good boy! I knew you'd do it. Again, now!"

The regulars scored another touchdown, but it took longer than the first. Insensibly the line in front of them was stiffening. The backs got into the game; the left wing, stirred by a touch of rivalry, perhaps, began to put a little snap into their work. By the time the regulars had forced the pigskin for the third time over their opponent's goal-line, the scrub seemed actually to be waking up. Vedder grumbled continually, but nevertheless he worked; many of the others blustered a bit to cover their change of tactics. It was as if they were doubtfully testing out Tompkins's statement that it was more fun to fight back than to be walked over, and finding an unexpected pleasure in the process.

Amazed at first, Sherman Ward lost no time in helping along the good work. After the third down he gave the scrub the ball and urged them to make the other fellows hustle. They took him up with a will. Saunders's perfunctory bark became snappy and full of life; more than one of the hitherto grouchy players added his voice to the general racket. But through it all, the good-natured urgence of Dale Tompkins, with that underlying note of perfect faith in their willingness to try anything, continued to stir the fellows to their best efforts.

The swiftly falling autumn twilight found the regulars fighting harder than they had ever done before to hold back the newly galvanized scrub. To the latter it brought a novel sensation. For the first time on record they were almost sorry to see the end of practice.

Streaking across the field to the shed which had been fixed up for a dressing-room, they laughed, and joked, and vehemently discussed the latter plays.

"Wait till to-morrow!" shrilly advised one of the scrub. "We won't do a thing to you guys, will we, Tommy?"

"That's the talk!" agreed Tompkins, smilingly. "We'll make 'em hump, all right."

He seemed quite unconscious of having done anything in the least out of the ordinary. On the contrary, he was filled with grateful happiness at the subtle change in the manner of many of the fellows toward him. It wasn't that they praised his playing. Except Sherman, who briefly commended him, no one actually mentioned that. But instead of Tompkins, they called him Tommy; they jollied and joshed him, argued and disputed and chaffed with a boisterous friendliness as if he had never been anything else than one of them. And the tenderfoot, hustling into his clothes that he might make haste to start out with his papers, glowed inwardly, responding to the treatment as a flower opens before the sun.

From the background Ranny Phelps observed it all with silent thoughtfulness. Quick-witted as he was, it did not take long for him to realize the changed conditions, to understand that he could not longer treat the new-comer with open, careless insolence as a fellow who did not count. But far from altering his opinion of Tompkins, the new developments merely served to strengthen his dislike, which speedily crystallized into a determination to do some active campaigning against him.

"With a swelled head added to all the rest, he'll be simply intolerable," decided Phelps. "I guess I've got a little influence left with the crowd in spite of all this rot." His eyes narrowed ominously as they rested on Harry Vedder chatting affably with the cause of Ranny's ill temper. "I'll start with you, my fat friend," he muttered contemptuously under his breath. "You need a good jacking-up before you indulge in any more foolishness."

CHAPTER V

TROUBLE AHEAD

In spite of all that had happened that day, Dale did not forget his appointment with Mr. Curtis. He hurried through supper, and pausing only to tell his mother where he was going, he slipped out of the house and started at a trot toward the scoutmaster's house. Mr. Curtis himself opened the door, greeted the boy cheerily, and ushered him into a room on the left of the hall, a room lined with books and pictures, with a fire glowing and sputtering on the hearth and some comfortable arm-chairs drawn up beside it.

"Well, young man," he said briskly as soon as Dale was seated, "I've been hearing things about you this afternoon."

Dale flushed, and his fingers unconsciously interlocked. The affair of the afternoon before had been "rubbed into him" at intervals all day, so that he almost dreaded further comment. It seemed as if it had been talked about quite enough and ought now be allowed to fall into oblivion. He hoped Mr. Curtis wasn't going to ask him to go over all the details again.

"You seem to have managed admirably," went on the scoutmaster, in a matter-of-face manner. "What I'd like to know, though, is how you, a tenderfoot of barely a week's standing, happened to be so well posted on electricity and insulation and all the rest of it?"

"It–it's in the handbook," explained Dale, haltingly.

"So it is," smiled the scoutmaster; "but it isn't a part of the tenderfoot requirements. I even doubt whether many second-class scouts would be up on it. Have you gone through the whole book as thoroughly?"

Dale leaned back in his chair more easily. "Oh no, sir, not all! But that part's specially interesting, and I–I like to read it."

"I see. Well, it was a good stunt–a mighty good stunt! It's the sort of thing true scouting stands for, and I'm proud of you." In his glance there was something that told a good deal more than the words themselves, but somehow Dale didn't mind that. "I suppose, though, you've been hearing nothing else all day and must be rather tired of it, so we'll go on to this drill business. This is only one feature of our work, and perhaps the least important since we're a nonmilitary organization. But it helps set a fellow up, it teaches him obedience and quick thinking, and is useful in a number of other ways, so we've included it in the program. The movements aren't intricate. Suppose you take that cane over in the corner, and I'll go through them with you."

Dale obeyed promptly, and, returning with the article in question, stood facing the scoutmaster, who had also risen. With the feeling of being under inspection, he had naturally taken a good position, shoulders back and chin up, and Mr. Curtis nodded approvingly.

"That's the idea!" he said. "With the command 'Attention!' you take practically that position, heels together, shoulders back, chin up, and eyes straight ahead. Hold the staff upright with the thumb and first two fingers of the right hand, one end on the ground and the upper part against your right shoulder. That's the attitude you return to after each one of the movements. Now let's try the first one."

There were not more than six or seven of these, and the scoutmaster's instructions were so clear and explicit that Dale wondered, with a touch of chagrin, how he could possibly have bungled so on the night of the meeting. In less than half an hour he had the different evolutions fixed firmly in his mind and the cane was laid aside.

"You'd better run through them every night for ten minutes or so until they come intuitively, without your having to stop and think," advised the scoutmaster. "The main thing is to put snap and ginger into it, so that the whole line moves as one. How did the football go? You were out, weren't you?"

"Yes, sir," the boy answered, his eyes lighting. "It was dandy! It's a crackerjack team, all right, and we're going to work like sixty to get that pennant."

"That's the idea!" smiled Mr. Curtis. He had returned to his chair, but the boy remained standing beside the table. "It will mean work to take the game from Troop One; they've a corking team, you know. But I think if– Won't you sit down again, or have you lessons to get?"

Dale hesitated. The pleasant room with its glinting fire was very tempting. He had glimpsed a number of interesting-looking old weapons and pieces of Indian beadwork, too, on the walls or arranged along the tops of the bookcases, which he would like to examine more closely. But, on the other hand, eight waiting problems in algebra and some stiff pages of grammar loomed up to dissuade him.

"Thank you very much, sir, but I guess I'd better not to-night," hc finally decided. "I haven't anything done yet for to-morrow."

"You must come again, then," smiled the scoutmaster. "I'm always glad to have you boys drop in, even when you haven't anything special to talk over. Good night; and good luck with the football. I may see you at practice to-morrow."

Dale found it hard to wait for that moment. He was devoted to football, and he had not really played in almost a year. Small wonder, therefore, that he looked forward eagerly to even humdrum practice. He did not propose to stay on the scrub if hard work and constant effort could lift him to something better. But even if he failed of advancement, he loved the game enough for its own sake to give to it unceasingly the best that was in him.

As the days passed it began to look as if the pleasure he got merely in playing and in the belief that his efforts contributed a little to the good of the team was to be his sole reward. All that week he played left tackle on the scrub, save for half an hour or so on Friday when Ward tried him at right half, only to return him presently to his former position.

But if Dale was disappointed, he did not show it. He told himself that it was too soon to expect anything else. Sherman would naturally wish to try him out in every way before making a change in the line-up. So the tenderfoot kept himself vigorously to the scratch, growing more and more familiar with the various formations and carefully studying the methods of the fellows opposite him.

It was this latter occupation which brought the first faint touch of uneasiness regarding the strength of the team at large. He could not be quite sure, for of course ordinary practice seldom brings out the best in a player, but it seemed as if the fellows were a bit lacking in unity and cohesion. Of one thing at least he grew certain before he had been on the scrub two days. Wilks, at left tackle, was hesitating and erratic, with a tendency to ducking, which would have been even more apparent but for the constant support and backing of Ranny Phelps. The latter seemed not only able to play his own position with dash and brilliancy, but also to lend a portion of his strength and skill to support the wavering tackle. Whenever it was possible, he contrived to take a little more than his share of buffeting in the forward plunge, to bear the brunt of each attack. There were times, of course–notably when Ranny himself carried the ball–that this was impossible, and then it was that Wilks's shrinking became unmistakable.

"He's got cold feet," decided Tompkins, with the mild wonder of one to whom the game had never brought anything but exhilaration and delight. "They must be mighty good friends for Phelps to help him out like that!"

He sighed a little wistfully. Ranny was letting no chance slip these days to show his disapproval of the newest member of the troop. There were others, too, who followed his example and treated the tenderfoot with marked coldness. Even stout Harry Vedder, though occasionally forgetting himself in the heat of play, lacked the good-natured friendliness of that first day. To be sure, these were far from being a majority. They included practically only the members of Ranny Phelps's own patrol; the others had apparently accepted Tompkins as one of the bunch and continued to treat him as such. But Dale's was a friendly nature, and it troubled him a little, when he had time to think about it, to be the object of even a passive hostility.

These moments, however, were few and far between. What with football every afternoon, with lessons and occasional studying for the second-class tests, to say nothing of his paper-route and some extra delivery-work he had undertaken to add to his "suit" money, his days were pretty full. Besides, that doubt as to the entire efficiency of the team continued to worry him much more than any small personal trouble.

On Saturday they played Troop Six, and Dale sat among the substitutes on the side-lines. It was an admirable chance for sizing up the playing of the team as a whole, and before the end of the second quarter his freckled forehead was puckered with worried lines. He had no fear of their losing the game. Their opponents had notoriously the weakest team in the entire scout league, and already two goals had been scored against it. The tenderfoot was thinking of next Saturday, and wondering more and more what sort of a showing the fellows would make then.

Earlier in the season, Dale had watched Troop One throughout an entire game, and even then he had noted their clever team-work. As individuals, perhaps, they might not match up to his own organization. There was no one quite to equal the brilliant Ranny Phelps, the clever quick-witted Ward, or the dependable Wesley Becker at full. But the boy knew football well enough to realize that in the long run it isn't the individual that counts. Freak plays, snatching at chance and the unexpected, may sometimes win a game, but as a rule they avail little against the spirit of cohesion when each fellow works shoulder to shoulder with his neighbor, supporting, backing up, subordinating himself and the thought of individual glory to the needs of the team. During the past week Dale had felt vaguely that it was just this quality Troop Five lacked. Now the certainty was vividly brought home, with all the advantages of a sharp perspective. The center, alone, seemed fairly strong and united, with Bob Gibson in the middle "Turk" Gardner at right guard, and Frank Sanson at left. But Sanson got no help at all from Wilks, who, in his turn, took everything from Ranny Phelps. Court Parker made an admirable quarter-back, and Ward and Becker played the game as it should be played. But Slater at right tackle and Torrance behind him made another pair who seemed to think more of each other and of their individual success than of the unity of the team. They were great chums, Dale reflected thoughtfully, and in Ranny Phelps's patrol. He wondered if that had anything to do with it. He wondered, too, whether Sherman realized the situation.

"But of course he does!" he muttered an instant later. "Isn't he always after them to get together, though sometimes it seems as if he might go for them a little harder? I–I hope they do–before it's too late."

But somehow he could not bring himself to be very confident. To pull together a team that has been playing "every man for himself" is one of the hardest things in the world. Defeat will often do it more thoroughly than anything, but, in their case, defeat would mean the loss of all they had been striving for. It would have been better had they been up against any other team to-day. Pushed hard and forced to fight for a slender victory, they might have realized something of their weakness. But the very ease with which goal after goal was scored brought self-confidence and cock-sureness instead of wisdom.

"I guess we'll grab that little old pennant, all right," Dale heard more than one declare in the dressing-room. "Why, those dubs actually scored a goal on Troop One!"

The boy wanted to remind them that this was at the very beginning of the season, and since then two of their best men had left Troop Six for boarding-school. But from a raw tenderfoot and inconsidered member of the scrub any such comment would savor of cheekiness, so he kept silent.

On Monday the practice started out in such a casual, perfunctory manner that Sherman suddenly stopped the play and lashed out, sparing nobody. He was white-hot, and not hesitating to mention names, he told them just what he thought of their smug complaisance, their careless, unfounded confidence.

"You fellows seem to think all you have to do is to show up on the field Saturday and the other crowd are going to take to cover!" he snapped. "You walk through the plays without an idea of team-work, or mutual support, or anything. That isn't football; it's just plain foolishness! Why, the lines are as full of holes as a colander–and you don't even know it! I tell you, unless we get together and stop those gaps and work for the team right, that game Saturday will be a joke."

He hesitated an instant, striving for self-control. When he went on, his tone was slightly moderated. "Come ahead, now, fellows; let's get into it and do the thing the way it should be done. We can if we only will."

Unfortunately, the appeal failed more or less because of its very force. Sherman's one fault as a captain was a certain leniency of disposition. He was a bit easy-going, and preferred to handle the fellows by persuasion rather than force. The latter did not realize that it wasn't the happenings of that day alone which had so roused his wrath, that these were only the culmination of all their shortcomings for weeks past, that they had been accumulating until the pressure became so great that an explosion had to come. A few of the players understood, but the very ones who needed his advice the most set down the outburst to whim or temper or indigestion. Either they airily ignored it, or else grew sullen and grouchy. In either case they failed to make a personal application of his words, and the situation remained practically unchanged.

CHAPTER VI

THE QUARREL

"Great cats and little kittens!" exclaimed Court Parker, stopping suddenly beside the flagpole on the green. "I certainly am a chump."

"Just as you say," grinned the tenderfoot. "I'd hate to contradict you. How'd you happen to find it out all by yourself, though?"

They were on their way to the scout meeting, and up to that moment had been deep in a serious discussion of the football situation. But Parker was not one to remain serious for very long at a stretch, so his sudden outbreak failed to surprise Dale, even though he might be ignorant of its cause.

"Why, I had it all planned to coach you up on the drill this week, so you could put one over on Ranny," explained the volatile youth, as they started on again; "but I clean forgot. Hang it all!"

Dale smiled quietly to himself. "I shouldn't wonder if I could get it to-night," he said briefly. "It's not so awful hard, is it?"

"N-n-o, but you know Ranny; he's sure to try and trip you up. Oh, well, no use crying over spilt milk! Just don't let him rattle you, and we'll have you letter-perfect by next meeting."

Dale's lips twitched again, but he made no further comment as they hurried along Main Street and turned in beside the church. It was with very different feelings from the last time that he entered the parish-house, hung up his cap, and joined one of the groups gathered in the meeting-room. He was still the only one present without a uniform, but to-night he wore his best suit, his hair was smooth and glistening, and he could almost see himself in the brilliant polish of his shoes. It all helped to increase his poise and the feeling of self-confidence his knowledge of the drill had given him.

Mr. Curtis was away that night, and Wesley Becker was in charge. The assistant scoutmaster was perfectly capable of conducting the meeting, but being only a year or two older than many of the boys, it was inevitable that discipline should tend to relax slightly. There were no serious infractions, of course; the fellows, as a whole, were too well trained and too much in earnest for that. But now and then a suppressed snicker followed the utterance of a whispered jest, and Wesley had occasionally to repeat his orders before they were obeyed with the snap and precision that invariably followed the commands of Mr. Curtis.

Dale was not one of the offenders, if such they could be called. In the beginning he was too intent on going through the newly acquired evolutions of the drill to have much thought for anything else. Later on, the behavior of Ranny Phelps took all his attention.

The leader of Wolf patrol was far from being in the best of humors. Perhaps the events of the afternoon had soured his temper; or possibly the mere sight of Tompkins standing erect at the end of the line made him realize that his efforts to put the tenderfoot in his place had been more or less of a failure. At any rate, when staves were distributed and the drill commenced, he at once renewed his nagging, critical attacks of the week before.

For a time Dale tried not to notice it, trusting that his careful, accurate execution of the manœuvers would in itself be enough to still the unjust criticism. But presently he began to realize that Phelps was deliberately blind to his improvement, and a touch of angry color crept into his face. In the next figure he made a minor slip, and a snicker from Wilks increased Dale's irritation.

"Take your time, Tompkins, by all means," urged Phelps, sarcastically, when Becker ordered a repetition of the movement. "Maybe by the end of the evening you'll be able to do one of the figures half-way right."

Dale's lips parted impulsively, but closed again without a sound issuing forth. A dull, smoldering anger began to glow within him, and one hand gripped his staff tightly. What right had Ranny Phelps to shame and humiliate him before the whole troop? He was doing his best, and he felt that the showing wasn't such a bad one for a fellow who had been in the troop little more than a week. Any decent chap would have understood this and made allowances, would even have helped him along instead of trying by every means in his power to make him fail. Dale's chin went up a trifle, and his teeth clenched. By a great effort he managed to hold himself in for the remainder of the drill, but the anger and irritation bubbling up inside resulted in several more errors. When the drill was over and the fellows stood at ease for a few minutes before starting some signal-work, Phelps strode over to the new recruit.

"What's the matter with you, Tompkins?" he said with cold sarcasm. "At this rate, you're likely to spend the whole winter getting a few simple stunts into your head."

Dale's eyes flashed. "It might not be a bad idea to learn a few of the scout laws yourself," he snapped back impulsively.

"What's that?"

Ranny's voice was cool and level, but his eyes had narrowed and a spot of color glowed on each cheek. The fellows near them suddenly pricked up their ears and turned curiously in their direction.

"I said it wouldn't be a bad idea for you to learn some of the scout laws," repeated Dale, heedless of everything save the anger and indignation surging up within him. "There's one about being friendly, and another that says a scout is helpful. Maybe you know them by heart, but I don't believe–"

"That'll do!" cut in Ranny, harshly. "I certainly don't need any advice from you on how to–"

"You mean you won't take any," interrupted Dale, hotly.

"Patrols, attention!" rang out Becker's voice sharply.

Neither of the boys paid any heed; it is doubtful whether they even heard him. Tight-lipped, with fists clenched, they glared at one another from eyes that snapped angrily. In another moment, however, Becker gripped Phelps tightly by the shoulder and whirled him around.

"Cut that out and go back to your place!" he said sternly. "I called for order."

Ranny glowered at him for a moment, and then, without a word, turned on his heel and strode back to the head of the line. In the hush that followed, Dale drew a long breath and swallowed hard. His face still burned, and the fingers of his right hand were stiff and cramped from the grip he had unconsciously maintained on his staff. With an elaborate attempt at nonchalance, he listened to Becker's directions about the signaling, but all the while he was wondering what the fellows thought of him and wishing, with increasing fervency, that he had kept his self-control instead of flaring up in that foolish way.

For the remainder of the evening Phelps seemed coolly oblivious of Dale's existence. He did not even glance at the tenderfoot, though on the way out the two stood for a moment within arm's-length in the entry. He had apparently quite recovered his composure, but there was a cold hardness about his mouth that brought a queer, unexpected pang to Tompkins.

Not for the world would he have acknowledged it to any one–even to Court, who, with several others, expressed unqualified approval of the way in which Ranny had been "set down." It is doubtful, even, had he been given a chance to live over the evening, if his conduct would have been any different. But there could be no question of his keen regret that instead of thawing Phelps's coolness by his increased proficiency at the drill, he had only succeeded in vastly increasing the boy's animosity.

On Wednesday afternoon Dale was made the unconscious cause of still further adding to Ranny's ire. After half an hour of play, Ward suddenly ordered Larry Wilks out of the line-up and told Tompkins to take his place.

At the command the tackle started, stared incredulously at Sherman, and then, with lowering brow and an exaggerated air of indifference, turned and walked deliberately off the field. For an instant Ranny stood silent, a deep red flaming into his face. Then he whirled impulsively on Ward.

"Are you crazy, Sherm?" he demanded hotly. "Why, you'll queer the whole team by sticking in a greenhorn only three days before the game."

"I don't agree with you," retorted Ward, curtly. He spoke quietly enough, but a faint twitching at the corners of his mouth showed that he was holding himself in with difficulty. "Wilks has had plenty of warnings, and has seen fit to disregard them utterly. Besides," his voice took in a harder tone as his eyes followed the departing player he had counted on using in the scrub, "I'd rather use anybody–little Bennie Rhead, even–than a fellow who shows the lack of spirit he does. Take your place, Tompkins. Frazer, shift over to right tackle on the scrub. Edwards, you come in and play left guard for to-day. Scrub has the ball."

Ranny Phelps bit his lip, glared ill-temperedly, and then subsided. Tompkins shifted over to the regulars, his mind a queer turmoil of delight at the advancement, and regret and apprehension at this new cause for bickering among the players. Practice was resumed, but there was a notable feeling of constraint among the fellows, which did not entirely pass off as the afternoon wore away. Ranny held himself coldly aloof, playing his own position with touches of the old brilliancy, but ignoring the chap beside him. Torrance and Slater, and one or two of the scrub who were part of the Phelps clique, whispered occasionally among themselves, or darted indignant glances at the tenderfoot as if he were in some way responsible for the downfall of Wilks. Dale tried not to notice it all, and devoted himself vigorously to playing the game, hoping that by the next day the fellows would cool down and get together.

But somehow they didn't. There had been time for discussion with the disgruntled Wilks himself, and if anything, their animosity was increased. It was so marked, and the effect so disastrous, or so it seemed to Tompkins, to the unity of the team, that after practice the tenderfoot hesitatingly approached Sherman Ward. It was not at all easy for him to say what he had in mind. For one thing, the idea of even remotely advising the captain savored of cheekiness and presumption; for another, he wasn't personally at all keen to take the step he felt would be for the good of the team. But at length he summoned courage to make the suggestion.

"Say, Sherm," he began haltingly, after walking beside Ward for a few moments in silence, "don't you think–that is, would it be better for me to–er–not to play to-morrow?"

Sherman stopped short in surprise. "Not play?" he repeated sharply. "Why, what–" He frowned suddenly. "Don't you want to?"

"Want to? Of course I do! But it seems to me things would–would go smoother if–I wasn't in the line-up. You know some of the fellows–"

He paused. Sherman's eyes narrowed. "Oh, that's what you mean, is it?" For an instant he stood staring silently at the freckled face raised to his. "You'd be willing to get out for–for the good of the team?" As Dale nodded he reached out and caught the boy almost roughly by one shoulder. "Forget it!" he said gruffly. "I know what I'm doing, kid. You go in to-morrow and play up for all you're worth. If–if those chumps don't come to their senses, it won't be your fault."

His jaw was square; his lips firm. It flashed suddenly on Dale that Sherman couldn't very well follow his suggestion and continue to preserve a shred of authority as captain. It would seem as if he were giving in to the delinquents and allowing them to run the team. They would set him down as weak and vacillating, and pay less attention than ever to his efforts to make them get together and play the game right. A sudden anger flamed up within the tenderfoot, and his teeth clicked together.

"Chumps!" he growled to himself, his fists clenching. "Can't they see what they're doing? Can't they forget themselves for a minute and think of the team?"

He wished the suspense was over and the moment for the game at hand. Hitherto the days had fairly flown, making the afternoons of much needed practice incredibly brief, but now the very minutes seemed to drag. Saturday morning was interminable. Dale tried to forget his worries by attending to the various chores about the house, but even in the midst of vigorous woodchopping he found himself stopping to think of the struggle of the afternoon, going over the different plays and sizing up the probable behavior of various individuals.

But at last the waiting was over and he had taken his place in that line which spread out across the field ready for the signal. And as he crouched there, back bent, watching with keen, appraising eyes the blue jersies dotting the turf before him, the tension relaxed a little, giving place to the thrall of the game.

After all, why should he be so certain of the worst? Wasn't it quite as likely that the fellows would be awakened and dominated, even stung into unity, by the same thrill which moved him? An instant later he lunged forward and was running swiftly, madly, his face upturned to the yellow sphere soaring above his head and rocking gently in its swooping, dropping flight.

When Ranny Phelps made a perfect catch and zigzagged down the field, dodging the interference with consummate skill, the tenderfoot thrilled responsive and mentally applauded. When the blond chap was at length downed and the teams lined up snappily, Dale grinned delightedly to himself at the realization of the fine beginning they had made.

But his enthusiasm was short-lived. Parker ripped out a signal, and the ball was snapped back to Ward. Dale drove forward, bent on clearing the way for Sherman. Beside him Ranny also lunged into the mêlée, but the tenderfoot was instantly conscious of a gap between them that seemed as wide as the poles apart. Into it the solid blue-jerseyed interference thrust itself, and the forward rush stopped as if it had struck a stone wall.

"First down!" shouted the referee when the heap of players disintegrated. "Ten yards to gain!"

CHAPTER VII

IN THE LAST QUARTER

As Dale scrambled to his feet and sought his place again, his face was flaming. He had a feeling that he must be partly to blame for the failure. Perhaps he had been a bit too quick in his forward lunge. As he crouched in the line, head low and shoulders bent, his hands clenched themselves tightly. It mustn't happen again, he told himself.

But swiftly it was borne upon him that the blame did not lie on his shoulders. A try around right end brought them barely a yard. Something had gone wrong there, too. He could not tell just what it was, but it seemed as if Slater and Torrance had failed somehow to back up Ted MacIlvaine as they should have done. The tackle's teeth grated, and a flood of impotent anger surged over him. They were playing as they had played in practice, each fellow for himself, without even an effort to get together and tighten up.

With the inevitable kick which gave the ball to Troop One, this fact became even more apparent. Solid and compact, the blue line swept down the field with a machine-like rush that carried everything before it. They seemed to find holes everywhere in the opposing line, and only the handicap of a high wind and the brilliant work of three or four individuals kept them from scoring in the first quarter.

That such a calamity could be long prevented seemed impossible to Dale. He greeted the intermission with a sigh of thankfulness. Brief as it was, it was a respite. Sherman's bitter, stinging onslaught on the team passed almost unheeded by the anxious tackle. He was thinking of the three remaining quarters with a foreboding that made him oblivious to all else.

To be sure, when play was resumed, the fellows seemed to show a slightly better spirit. It was as if the first dim realization of their errors was being forced upon them. But they had been split apart so long that they seemed to have forgotten how to work together in that close-knit, united manner which alone could make any head against these particular opponents. Time and time again they were driven back to the very shadow of their goal-posts, where, stung by shame or the lashing tongue of their captain, they rallied long enough to hurl back the attack a little, only to lapse again when the pressing, vital need was past.

Then, toward the very end of that second quarter, when Tompkins was just beginning to hope again, the thing he had dreaded came suddenly and unexpectedly. Some one blundered, whether Slater, or Torrance, or Ted MacIlvaine, the boy did not know. With a last swift rush the blue-clad interference charged at the right wing, through it, over it, and, hurling aside all opposition, swept resistlessly over the last six yards for a touchdown. They missed the goal by a hair, but that did not lessen the sense of shock and sharp dismay which quivered through the line of their opponents.

Dale Tompkins took his place after the long intermission, a dull, bitter, impotent anger consuming him. He was furious with the fellows who by their incredible stupidity were practically throwing away the game. He even hated himself for seeming to accomplish so little; but most of all he raged at the blond chap next to him. Some of the others were at least trying to get together, though their lack of practice made the effort almost negligible. But Ranny Phelps remained as coldly aloof, as markedly determined to withhold support and play his game alone as he had been in the beginning.

It made a hole in the line which could not escape the attention of the opposing quarter-back. Already he had sent his formation through it more than once, but now he seemed to concentrate the attack on that weak spot. Time and time again Dale flung himself to meet the rush, only to be overwhelmed and hurled back by sheer numbers. Sometimes Sanson pulled him out of the scrimmage, more often he scrambled up unaided to find his place, sweat-blinded and with breath coming in gasps, and brace himself for the next onset.

Silently, doggedly, he took his punishment, and presently, under the strain, he began to lose track of the broader features of the game. Vaguely he realized that they had been forced back again and again almost against their own goal-posts, and there had rallied, tearing formations to shreds and hurling back the enemy with the strength of despair. Dimly he heard the voice of Ward, or Court Parker's shriller notes, urging them in sharp, broken phrases to get together. But the real, the dominating thing was that forward plunge, the tensing of muscles, the crash of meeting bodies, the heaving, straining struggle, the slow, heartrending process of being crushed back by overwhelming weight–that and the sense of emptiness upon his left.

Then came a time when things went black for an instant before his eyes. He did not quite lose consciousness, for he knew when the weight above was lifted and two arms slid around him, dragging him to his feet. It was Sanson, he thought hazily–good old Frank! Then he turned his head a little and through the wavering mists looked straight into the eyes of Ranny Phelps!

Wide, dilated, almost black with strain and excitement, they stared at him from out the grimy face with a strange mingling of shame and admiration that sent a thrill through the tenderfoot and made him pull himself together.

"Take it easy," came in gruff, unnatural accents. "You want to get your wind–old fellow."

"I–I'm all right," muttered the tenderfoot.

He passed one hand vaguely across his forehead. Some one brought a tin dipper, from which he rinsed his mouth mechanically. His head was clearing, but he couldn't seem to understand whether the transformation in the chap beside him was real or only a creation of his bewildered brain. But when he took his place again and dropped his shoulders instinctively, another shoulder pressed against him on the left, and that same hoarse, unfamiliar voice sounded in his ears:

"Together now, kid; we'll stop 'em this time!"

The words seemed to give Dale a new strength. Stirred to the very fiber of his being, he dived forward to meet the onward rush. Still with that new, stimulating sense of support where none had been before, his outstretched hands gripped like tentacles around sturdy legs. There was a heaving, churning motion; then the compact mass of players toppled over, and he knew that they had succeeded.

Nor was it a solitary advantage. Unobserved by Tompkins, the whole line had been slowly stiffening. Slowly, gradually, the other holes had been closed up and the advance checked. When the kick put the ball in their possession, a new spirit animated Troop Five. Scattered no longer, but welded by stern necessity into a single unit, they forgot their handicap, forgot that the minutes of the final quarter were speeding in mad flight, forgot everything but the vital need of breaking through that line of blue and carrying the fight toward those distant goal-posts that loomed so far away.

Forming up swiftly, they swept forward for a gain of eight yards. Before the opposition recovered from their surprise, they had passed the fifty-yard line.

Here the blues rallied, and for a space the two lines surged back and forth in the middle of the field. It was a period of small gains and frequent punts, when neither side held the ball long, nor the advantage. Thrilled by their success, exhilarated by that strange new sense of comradeship with the boy beside him, Dale fought fiercely, heedless of the shock of bodies, of pain, of weariness, of blinding sweat, or hard-won breath. His only worry was a growing fear that they would not have time to score, and this had only just begun to dominate him when the unexpected happened.

They were battling on the enemy's forty-yard line. It was Troop One's ball, and they had tried to force a gain through center. Shoulder to shoulder, Ranny and Dale plunged forward to meet the rush. The advance checked, Tompkins gained his feet swiftly and thrilled to see the precious ball rolling free not a dozen feet away.

With a gasp he lunged for it and scooped it up without slackening speed. At almost the same instant Ranny Phelps shot out of the scrimmage as if propelled from a catapult, and a moment later the two were thudding down the field, a stream of players trailing in their wake.

Dale caught his breath with the stinging realization that their chance had come–their only chance! There were but two men between them and the coveted goal, the full-back, and nearer, another player bearing swiftly down on them, who must instantly be reckoned with. That would be Ranny's task. He must stop the fellow, while Dale took his chance alone with the other.

Dale glanced sideways at his companion, and his heart leaped into his throat. Phelps was limping; something had happened to him in that last scrimmage. His face showed white even through the grime and tan; his under lip was flecked with crimson.

"Ranny!" gasped Dale, in a panic. "What– Can you–"

"Don't–worry–about–me," came indistinctly through the other's clenched teeth. "I'll–block–this fellow–somehow. You get the other–you've got to!"

Taking a fresh grip on the ball, Dale spurted on. He was aware that Ranny had sheered off a little to the right, and knew that he meant to stop the boy racing up from that direction. But actually he saw nothing, and even the crash of meeting bodies came to him as something far away and unimportant. His clearing brain was fixed on the looming figure ahead, the full-back, who alone stood between him and victory.

He must be passed–but how? A thought of hurdling flashed into his mind, to be dismissed as too hazardous. There was only one way left. Without slackening speed, he tore on, his heart thumping like a trip-hammer. To the breathless onlookers it seemed as if he meant actually to run down the opposing player. Then, in a flash, when he was almost within reach of the hooking arms, he swerved suddenly to one side, whirled, darted the other way, eluded the other's frantic clutch by the merest hair, and with a sob of joy ran on, free, the ball still cupped in the curve of his arm.

CHAPTER VIII

THE GOOD TURN

Ten minutes later the small building on the edge of the field was thronged with joyous, excited boys in various stages of undress, who celebrated the victory with shrill jubilations, snatches of song, or exuberant outbursts of mere noise. The strain and tension of the afternoon were forgotten; nobody remembered the nearness of defeat in the recollection of that last splendid rally which had brought them all so much closer together.

On every hand fellows were comparing notes and talking over details of the struggle in eager fragments. "Remember the time–" "Say, how about that gain through center when Ted–" "Some run, wasn't it?"

"Oh, you Tommy!" shrilled Court Parker, catching Dale's eye. "Awful punk run that was–simply awful!"

Tompkins smiled back at him, but did not speak. He was luxuriating in the restful peace which comes after strenuous physical action and the consciousness of successful accomplishment. A feeling of intense pride in the troop filled him. "They're a corking lot of fellows–corking!" he said more than once under his breath as he looked around the room with shining eyes. "How they did get after that bunch in the last quarter! I–I wouldn't belong to any other troop for–for anything!"

Now and then, to be sure, his eyes strayed to the farther end of the room, where Ranny Phelps was having his swollen ankle bandaged by two of the most skilful exponents of first aid, and a faint touch of questioning crept into them. Since that breathless moment on the field when Ranny's efforts had left the way free for Dale, he had not spoken to the tenderfoot nor by so much as a glance recognized his existence. Dale wondered whether his mind was merely taken up with his injury, or whether the change that had come over him in the heat of the game had been only a temporary thawing.

As the days passed, the latter suspicion became a certainty. At their very first meeting, in fact, the tenderfoot found Ranny as aloof as ever. To be sure, Dale noticed that he no longer seemed to try to impress his attitude on the others in his patrol. Apparently without rebuke, stout Harry Vedder became quite friendly, and even Rex Slater and one or two others in the clique treated him with a good deal more consideration than they had before the game. But the leader himself made no effort to disguise his coolness toward the new-comer, and Dale presently found it hard to believe that the helping hand, the friendly voice, the touch of that muscular shoulder as they fought side by side on the field in the furious struggle against odds had been real.

He did not brood over it, because he was not of the brooding sort. More than once he found himself regretting that impulsive action which had so increased the other boy's antagonism, but for the most part he contented himself with the unqualified friendship of most of the troop, and entered with zest into the various scout activities.

Perhaps the most interesting of these were the long hikes and week-end camping-trips. Mr. Curtis was a great advocate of the latter, and as soon as the end of football made Saturdays free again, he announced his intention of undertaking them as often as the weather permitted.

Unfortunately, there were not many sites around Hillsgrove which combined the ideal qualifications for a camp–good drainage, wood, and water. The latter was particularly scarce. There were one or two brooks–small, miserable affairs with only a foot or two of depth, and a muddy, half-stagnant mill-pond or so; but the single body of water which would have been perfect for the purpose was definitely and permanently barred to them.

It was a small lake, half a mile long and varying from two to four hundred feet in width, that lay some four miles out of town. There was a good bottom, depth in plenty even for diving, and the banks on one side, at least, sloped back sharply and were covered with a fine growth of pine and hemlock, interspersed with white birch and a good deal of hard wood. The boys had often looked on it with longing eyes, but the owner was a sour-faced, crotchety old man who was enraged by the mere sight of a boy on his property. He had placarded his woods with warning signs, kept several dogs, and was even reputed to have a gun loaded with bird-shot ready for instant use on youthful trespassers.

Perhaps the latter was a slight exaggeration; certainly no one had ever been actually peppered with it. But the fact remained that old Caleb Grimstone, who lived alone and had a well-established reputation for crankiness, had stubbornly refused all requests to be allowed to camp or picnic on his property even when pay was offered, and at length all such effort had been abandoned. As Court Parker remarked, no doubt with a vivid recollection of sundry narrow escapes: "You can steal a swim on the old codger if you keep a weather-eye peeled and don't mind doing a Marathon through the brush; but when it comes to anything like pitching a tent and settling down–good night!"

Under such circumstances, it may be imagined that the announcement made one morning to the group gathered about the school entrance that old Grimstone had fallen through the hay-shoot and broken an arm did not elicit any marked expressions of regret.

"Serves him right, the old skinflint, after the mean way he's kept us away from the lake!" growled Bob Gibson.

"Yes, indeed!" sniffed Harry Vedder. "He's a regular dog in the manger. It wouldn't hurt him to let us swim there in the summer, or camp once in a while. He doesn't use it himself."

"Use it!" exclaimed Frank Sanson. "Why, they don't even cut ice off it."

"He's just downright mean, that's all!" put in Rex Slater. "Say, fellows, what a chance this would be to get ahead of the old chap and camp out Friday or Saturday–if Mr. Curtis would only let us."

"He won't," said Sherman Ward, decidedly. "Besides, it's a lot too cold and looks like snow. How did he manage, Ted? Living alone with only those dogs, it must have been some stunt to get word to anybody."

"He got out to the road and waited for the first team that came along," explained Ted. "The people took him into the house, and then sent Dr. Maxwell out from town. He wanted somebody to come and look after him, but old Grimey wouldn't hear of it. Said he couldn't stand the expense."

"The old miser! How does he manage to get his meals and look after the stock?"

"Eats bread and milk and canned stuff, I guess. Bud Hinckley comes in night and morning, I understand, to look after the horse and cow and wash dishes and all that, but you know what Bud is."

"So lazy he'd like somebody else to draw his breath for him!" said Court Parker, promptly. "Whew! What a lovely time the old man must be having–and to-morrow Thanksgiving!"

As they trooped into school, the last words lingered in Dale Tompkins's mind. To-morrow would, indeed, be Thanksgiving–the day of turkey, and mince-pie, and good cheer generally. He had no more cause than the others for sympathizing with Caleb Grimstone, but somehow the mental picture of the soured old man sitting alone in his slovenly kitchen, one arm in a sling, and eating bread and milk, with perhaps a can of lukewarm tomatoes or corn, when every one else was feasting merrily in company, made him vaguely uncomfortable.

He forgot it, however, in the excitement of a brisk game of land-hockey up at Sherman's that afternoon, but after supper the picture returned with renewed vividness, and with it something the scoutmaster had said when he passed his second-class examinations a few days ago.

"Never forget the daily good turn, Dale, or let it slump into a perfunctory sort of thing such as you would have to do anyway whether you were a scout or not. A fellow can't always find big things, of course; but when the opportunity comes, he isn't a true scout if he cannot sacrifice his own comfort or pleasure or inclination to bring help or happiness to some one who really needs it."

Dale squirmed a little at the recollection and tried to go on with the book he was reading. But the tale had lost its savor, and presently he raised his eyes from the printed page and frowned.

"Nobody else thought anything about it!" he muttered rebelliously. "Besides, to-morrow's Thanksgiving; that's different from any other day."

A little later he put away the book, said good night, and went up to his room. Having closed the door, he opened his closet and took out his scout suit. It had come only the day before; already he had looked at it more than twenty times, but the novelty had not yet worn off. He wondered if fellows who had theirs merely for the asking felt half as proud of it as he, who had worked for every penny of its cost. He passed one hand caressingly over the smooth olive khaki, and then an odd thought popped suddenly into his head.

He had tried it on, twice, but as yet he had not actually worn it. Mightn't it mean even more to him if he wore it first in the performance of a good turn that really counted?

Though the boy felt it only vaguely, and formulated it not at all even in his mind, it was something of that spirit of consecration that of old dominated the young candidates for knighthood, guarding their armor through the long night-watches. Dale's face took on an expression of determination, and as he put away his things his mind was oddly lightened.

Next morning he sallied forth, a trifle self-conscious in all the glory of his new khaki, but warmed by the look in his mother's eyes as she waved good-by from the door-step. Taking the shortest cut, he proceeded to the rectory, and when Mr. Schofield appeared he saluted punctiliously.

"May I have one of the baskets, sir?" he asked.

The rector smiled. "Ah! You're going to take it to–" He paused questioningly an instant; then his smile deepened. "Certainly," he said cordially. "They're over in the parish-house. The ladies are packing them now. Tell Mrs. Mason I said you were to have a good one."

Ten minutes later Dale was making his way briskly toward the Beldon Turnpike, a large market-basket on one arm. The legs of a plump fowl protruded from the covering; there were vegetables within, a can of soup, celery, oranges, bananas, and a small pie. The weight was not a light one, but Dale whistled cheerfully as he strode along.

He reached the turnpike without meeting any of the fellows, and after ten or fifteen minutes' tramping along the straight, level road he paused to shift the basket to the other arm. It was heavier than he thought. Overhead the gray sky was a bit dispiriting, and the sharp, chill wind, blowing across the open fields, made him glad he had buttoned his sweater beneath the khaki coat.

Presently he began to speculate on what sort of reception he would have, and for the first time the possibility occurred to him that his welcome might not be altogether cordial. You never could tell what point of view the cranky old man would take. He thought of the dogs, too, especially after he had left the main road and turned into the less frequented one leading past Grimstone's place. More than once people had been chased by them, and it wasn't exactly pleasant to picture them rushing out at him in a body the moment he set foot in the lane.

Nevertheless, it did not occur to him to turn back. He had set out with a definite purpose, and he meant to carry it through. To be sure, just before reaching the lane he cut himself a stout stick, and as the old, weather-beaten frame house came in sight he unconsciously made his approach as noiseless as possible. He was surprised and not a little relieved to see no signs of the animals, but when he set down his basket and knocked briskly on the back door, the snarling uproar that instantly arose inside plainly advertised their whereabouts.

Dale tightened his grip on the stick and strained his ears for other sounds. He had raised his hand for a second knock when the barking suddenly lessened a little, and above the racket came a growling admonition in Grimstone's harsh tones:

"Wal, come in, can't you? Are you deaf?"

CHAPTER IX

AN ODD THANKSGIVING

The note of ill temper in the voice was so apparent that Dale hesitated for a second longer. Then, with a determined movement of his head, he set his stick against the door-casing, picked up the basket, and stepped into the kitchen. It was a long, low room, the walls and ceiling painted a dirty gray. Two of the three windows were tightly shuttered, so that Dale could barely make out the bent figure seated in a rocking-chair beside a rusty, decrepit cook-stove. At his entrance the three dogs began to bark again, but old Grimstone silenced them with a fierce gesture that sent them cowering under a table.

"What d' you want?" he demanded, glaring at the boy from under bushy brows. "I don't want to buy nothin', so you'd better git out."

"I haven't anything–for sale," returned the boy, finding it a little difficult to explain his errand. "It–it's your Thanksgiving dinner."

"Dinner!" snapped the old man. "What are you talkin' about? I ain't ordered nothin' from town."

"I know you haven't. It's one of the baskets from the church. I–I heard you'd had an accident and were all alone, so I–I thought I'd bring it out."

For a moment the old man sat silent, his hard, glinting eyes, full of sour suspicion, fixed on the boy's face. "What for?" he demanded suddenly.

"What for?" repeated Dale, puzzled.

"Yes; what for? What d' you expect to git out of it? You ain't toted a basketful o' truck all the way out here jest out of regard for me, I reckon. Who sent ye?"

Dale flushed, and unconsciously drew himself up a little. "Nobody," he returned briefly. "I'm a boy scout. We–we try to do a good turn for somebody every day."

Old Grimstone bent slightly forward, staring in a puzzled fashion at the trim, khaki-clad figure before him. His right arm, bulky with bandages and splints, was strapped tightly to his body; the other hand, gnarled and brown, with blue veins showing here and there, gripped the arm of the rocker. There was suspicion still in his glance, but back of it was the look of one groping dimly for something he could not understand. Suddenly he straightened with a jerk.

"Wal, set it down somewheres, then!" he growled ungraciously. "I ain't an object o' charity yet, but if you're bound to leave it, I s'pose I can use it somehow. You'd better be startin' back right away or you'll miss your dinner."

Dale placed the basket on a table and commenced to remove the paper. "I'm not going back yet," he explained cheerfully. "I'm going to stay and cook it for you."

For a moment there was silence. Then the old man grunted inarticulately; it might have been with surprise, or incredulity, or almost any other emotion. Dale's back was toward him, so he could not tell, but since there was no actual prohibition, he proceeded with the unpacking.

Somehow he was beginning to enter more into the spirit of the thing, beginning to feel an interest, almost an enjoyment, in doing it up thoroughly. Having taken off coat and sweater, his first act was to prepare the chicken for roasting. When it was safely placed in the oven he shook down the fire, added some more wood, and then turned his attention to a pile of unwashed dishes, which the indolent Hinckley was evidently accumulating until he considered it sizeable enough to be worth tackling. It was a task the boy ordinarily hated, but he meant to leave the room spick and span on his departure. So he rolled up his shirt-sleeves and plunged in, whistling softly as he worked.

"What d'you want?" he demanded

Old Caleb Grimstone followed the boy's movements almost in silence. He had gruffly told him where he could find a pan for the chicken, and once he snapped out at one of the dogs who had come forth from under the table and was sniffing at Dale's legs. But for the most part he sat motionless beside the stove, his eyes, under their beetling brows, fixed intently on the busy figure with that same puzzled questioning in their depths.

At last, when Dale had pared the potatoes and put them on to boil, he suddenly growled, "Are you one of them boys that come sneakin' around the lake last summer?"

Dale reddened a little, but did not hesitate. "I was out here two or three times, I guess," he acknowledged.

The old man sniffed. "I s'pose you call that one o' them 'good turns'–trespassin' on a person's property, an' payin' no attention to signs, an' all," he remarked.

"I wasn't a scout then," said Dale. He got a broom from the corner, and on his way past the old man's chair he paused, his eyes twinkling a bit. "Anyhow, on a roasting hot day you know a fellow'll do 'most anything to get a swim. I expect you were that way yourself, Mr. Grimstone, when you were a boy."

"Huh!" grunted the old man, disagreeably, but he made no further comment.

Once or twice, as he swept, Dale glanced curiously at the silent figure by the stove and wondered what the old fellow was thinking about. His eyes no longer followed the boy with sharp suspicion. His head was bent a little, and he stared blankly, unseeingly, at a knot in the board at his feet. For a long time he did not stir, save once to lift the thin, veined hand from the chair-arm, only to grip it again with a force that made the knuckles stand out white against the brown skin. At length, with a sigh, checked almost in its birth, he raised his head and frowned at Tompkins.

"Ain't you goin' to baste that fowl at all?" he inquired sharply.

Dale started guiltily at the reminder and hastened to the oven. The fowl was browning nicely, and as he spooned up the sizzling juices, he hoped his forgetfulness wasn't going to make any difference in its flavor.

Apparently it hadn't. After a number of anxious inspections, between which he set the table for two, put plates to heat, and arranged the remaining contents of the basket as temptingly as he could, he decided that the chicken was done, and Mr. Grimstone, peering doubtfully into the oven and even testing the fowl with a fork, grudgingly agreed. When the old man was served and his portion cut up so that he could manage it with a fork, Dale took his first taste with a little feeling of pride in his culinary achievement.

It was really a very appetizing meal, and the scout enjoyed it as only a healthy, hungry boy can. Mr. Grimstone made no comment one way or another. Once or twice he mumbled his annoyance at having to have his meat cut up for him by a boy, but the number of times that the process was repeated and the relish with which he consumed everything in sight was proof enough of his satisfaction in the unwonted fare.

As the curious meal proceeded to its conclusion he seemed almost to thaw a little. His manner was still crabbed and his voice sharp. He scowled a good deal, too, especially after some comment which might possibly be taken as approaching the amiable. But in one way or another, both at table and later while the dishes were being done up, he asked a good many questions in his short, snappy fashion.

Dale answered them readily, vaguely sensing, perhaps, that under the old man's surface crustiness lay a certain awkwardness at handling so unaccustomed a situation. After all these years of bitter warfare against boys it must be rather embarrassing, he thought, to treat one of them with even an approach to civility. So when he had told his name, and the troop he belonged to, and one or two other details the old man asked about, Dale went on to explain a little about their scout work and play, their weekly meetings and drill and other duties, their hikes and week-end camping-trips.

The old man listened almost without comment. He seemed more curious about the principle of the daily good turn, to which he reverted several times, always with expressions of doubt and skepticism. The idea of mere boys giving time and labor and sacrificing inclination and pleasure without thought of reward was incredible to him.

"It ain't natural!" he declared at last. "Mebbe one or two might, but not many. You can't tell me any other o' them young limbs in town would of give up their holiday to tote a basket o' truck out here an' cook it."

"Oh, yes, they would!" protested the boy, loyally, "if they'd thought of it."

"Humph!" grunted the old man. "They didn't happen to, though."

"One was enough, wasn't it?" smiled the boy. "You wouldn't have known what to do with two baskets."

The old man snorted doubtfully and did not pursue the subject farther. A little later, Dale discovered, to his surprise, that it was after four. He had no idea the time had flown so. He would have to hustle to get back to town before dark. Fortunately, the kitchen was cleared up, so after stoking the fire he got into his sweater and coat. Then he picked up the wide-brimmed felt hat and carefully rearranged the depressions in its crown.

"Good-by, Mr. Grimstone," he said, glancing over to where the latter had resumed his place by the stove. "I hope your arm won't be long coming around."

The old man frowned at him from under the bushy brows. His head was a little bent, and the long, bony fingers curved over the chair-arm. It was precisely the attitude with which he had greeted the boy's arrival; yet the latter was conscious of a subtle, intangible difference, felt rather than perceived.

"Good-by," he answered curtly. That was all until Dale reached the door and was turning the knob. Then, "Much obleeged," came jerkily from the thin, straight lips.

"You needn't be," smiled the scout. "I–I've had a very good time."

It was not exactly the polite fiction that perhaps it seemed. That was the odd part of it. As he went briskly down the lane the boy realized with surprise that not once had he thought regretfully of the rare turkey-dinner at home, or the fun with the fellows he had missed that afternoon. One of the dogs, still licking his chops from the dish of scraps that Dale had given them in the shed, trotted after him, and the boy bent to pat his head without a touch of nervousness.

"Your bark's a lot worse than your bite, old fellow," he said aloud.

He straightened up and glanced back at the rambling, weather-beaten house, whose roof lines seemed to merge into the cold gray of the sky, and something deeper than pity stirred him at the thought of the old man sitting alone there in the twilight.

"I shouldn't wonder if he was a good deal like his dogs," he murmured as he turned away. "I'm sort of glad–I found it out."

It was quite dark before Dale reached home. The return trip had been much harder to make than the one that morning. The holiday was over and there was no spirit of adventure to buoy him up, no consciousness that he was going to be of use to some one who needed him. Also, there was plenty of time to think of the good cheer he had missed at home–that family feast to which, as long as he could remember, they had sat down at three o'clock on Thanksgiving afternoon. It had become so fixed and seemingly immovable that Dale had not even considered the possibility of changing it. And so it was with a tired and lagging step that he walked up from the gate and opened the front door.

Inside, he paused suddenly and sniffed. For an instant he stood stock-still, eyes wide, mouth half open. Then, with a sudden, incoherent exclamation, he tore down the hall, past the lighted dining-room, and through the open kitchen door. The room was warm and bright, and filled with the delicious odor of roasting turkey.

"Mother!" he cried, his face shining. "You didn't have it– You–you–waited!"

His mother straightened from closing the oven door and smiled at him–that wonderful, indescribable smile that somehow belongs to mothers.

"Of course I waited!" she said quietly. Then, as he leaped forward and clutched her in a bear-hug, she laughed softly and asked, just a little tremulously, "Didn't you think Father and I could do a good turn, too?"

CHAPTER X

THE SURPRISE

There was no school on the Friday after Thanksgiving, and as soon as Dale had finished his chores he sallied forth to hunt up some of the fellows. A light snow had fallen during the night, but the day was clear and bright and just the sort for a good active game or a brisk hike. As he skirted the north side of the green a shrill yodeling from behind brought the scout around to see Court Parker bearing down upon him, calling out:

"Say, where were you yesterday, anyhow? I didn't see you all day."

"I was–busy," returned Dale, briefly.

"Busy stuffing yourself, I s'pose. Well, you missed a dandy game up at Sherm's. We're going to have another this afternoon."

"Won't the snow– Say! Why couldn't we play 'Smugglers over the Border,' or something like that? It's just the day for it."

Court's glance swept comprehensively over the snow-covered green and his eyes brightened. "I hadn't thought of that. Now and then you do manage to hit the little black circle, Tommy. Let's hunt up the bunch and see what they say."

The crowd was presently gathered from several different parts of town, and the majority approved of Dale's suggestion. Ranny Phelps and several of his clique had other plans for the afternoon, but Ranny had a habit of frequently failing to take part in the troop doings, unless these were official and gave him a chance to appear in uniform, girded with authority, so his absence was not unexpected.

Immediately after lunch the others betook themselves a mile outside of town, sides were chosen, and the "border" laid out. This consisted of about four hundred yards of a little-used road where the snow had not been much disturbed. This was patrolled by a portion of the "custom inspectors," with a reserve posted farther inland. About half a mile back from the road a deserted barn did duty for the "town."

The smugglers gathered about half a mile on the other side of the border and were allowed to cross it in any formation, singly, together, or scattered, and make for the town at any speed they chose. One only of their number was supposed to be smuggling, and he was equipped with tracking-irons. The moment a sentry patrolling the border caught sight of these tracks, his duty was to signal the fact to the reserve party of inspectors and at once follow the track himself. The reserves coöperated with him, trying by any means to catch the smuggler before he could reach the town. If they succeeded, the game was theirs; but if the smuggler eluded them and reached the barn safely, victory went to the other side.

It was a typical scout sport, and for three hours or more the fellows played it strenuously, varying it toward the end with one or two other stalking games. These all met with unanimous approval, even Bob Gibson, the habitual grumbler, admitting that it was more fun than he thought it would be.

"We'll have to try some more of those in the book," Ward remarked as they tramped back through the twilight. "That deer-hunt one sounds pretty good, if you fellows will only make bows and arrows enough. I vote we fix up a deer and go to it next Saturday."

It happened, however, that the following Saturday was devoted to something even more interesting than deer-hunting. As Dale entered the parish-house on Monday evening he passed Mr. Curtis, just inside the door, talking earnestly with Wesley Becker.

"It was a big surprise to me, I can tell you," he heard the scoutmaster say. "I can't imagine what has brought about the transformation."

"He doesn't say, I suppose?" asked Becker.

"No; it's just the curt invitation. He's hedged it about with all sorts of prohibitions, but still it's wonderful he should have come around at all."

"It'll be corking for the troop!" exclaimed Becker, enthusiastically. "That's the one thing we've lacked, and if–"

At that point Tompkins passed beyond the range of their voices, but he had heard enough to rouse his curiosity. Fortunately this did not have to remain long unsatisfied. After the opening exercises the scoutmaster faced the three patrols, a small sheet of paper in one hand.

"Attention, scouts!" he said crisply. "The troop will be much pleased to learn, I'm sure, that Mr. Grimstone has given us permission to use the north side of his lake for camping purposes."

For an instant there was amazed silence. Then a bedlam of surprised comment arose, mingled with a torrent of eager questions, which Mr. Curtis did not attempt to quell.

"Well, what do you know about that!" "Hurrah for old Grimey!" "Can we skate there, Mr. Curtis?" "Will he let us swim in the summer?" "Can't we go out this Saturday?" "How did you work it, sir?"

"One at a time," smiled the scoutmaster. "I'll answer the last one first. I didn't 'work it,' as you so pithily express it, Vedder, at all. I've failed several times to get this privilege from Mr. Grimstone, and his letter this morning was as much of a surprise to me as to any one. He doesn't state the reason for his change of mind."

A shock of sharp surprise sent the blood tingling into Dale Tompkins's face and clenched his hands spasmodically. "Gee!" he muttered under his breath. "I wonder– Why, it must be! But I never thought of that–not for a minute!" He paused an instant, his gaze growing introspective. "He certainly is one good old scout," he murmured to himself. "I said his bark was a lot worse than his bite."

Then he realized that Mr. Curtis was speaking.

"We're not to go beyond the dam at one end of the lake or the inlet at the other. In other words, there must be no trespassing on the side of the water where the buildings and orchard stand. He doesn't wish any timber cut, and there are several other minor prohibitions. He says nothing against swimming or skating, so I imagine both will be allowed. As for camping there on Saturday, I'm afraid it will be too cold to stay overnight, but there's no reason why we shouldn't hike out in the morning and make a day of it."

So it was that the following Saturday morning found practically the entire troop hiking briskly along the Beldon Turnpike at an early hour. Ranny Phelps had complained that there wouldn't be much fun in just a picnic affair, but he was there, nevertheless. The others had no such criticism to make. They fairly bubbled enthusiasm, and in their eagerness to reach the hitherto forbidden spot many of them would have willingly gone the entire distance at scout's pace.

When they finally left the road and turned off into the woods along an overgrown lumber-track, it was like exploring an undiscovered country. Most of them had been there before, but with a difference. When one's ears must be constantly open for the baying of dogs, with the necessity ever present of being ready for instant flight, there is little chance to appreciate the beauties of nature. Now, instead of having to creep along through trees and undergrowth, they could boldly follow the shore-line, investigate every little cove or promontory, discuss possible camping-sites, and even make definite plans with the assurance that these could be actually carried out in the spring.

At about eleven o'clock they reached the old swimming-place near the head of the lake and halted by general consent. Hitherto, they had considered the spot solely from the point of view of aquatic sport; now they realized that a more ideal spot for a camp could scarcely be imagined. A small, rocky point thrust its flat nose out into the lake. One side was sliced off as with a knife, and here the depth varied from six to eight feet; on the other it shelved more gradually. Back of it, the level open space, facing south and hedged in by a thick shelter of hemlock, would accommodate five or six shelter-tents with ease. Scarcely a dozen yards away, a clear spring bubbled into a mossy basin.

In an instant packs were laid aside, and under Becker's direction one party foraged for wood while another brought stones for an oven and cut saplings for the crane or forked sticks to use in broiling meat. Sandwiches and other ready-to-eat provisions were not looked upon with favor. Every boy wanted something he could cook, and the variety of chops, small steaks, eggs, bacon, ham, and the like that swiftly appeared was endless. One enterprising scout had even brought a can of twist-dough and proceeded deftly to brown it on sticks held over the embers. On every hand were voiced regrets that they couldn't have come prepared to stay overnight.

"I don't believe it would have been too cold, with the fire and everything," said Bennie Rhead, after they had finished luncheon and were sitting lazily around the blaze for a bit before tackling the job of cleaning up. "Why, it's as warm as toast now."

"Naturally, with the sun pouring in here all the morning," smiled Mr. Curtis. "You'd find it rather different at night. If we all had sleeping-bags or tents that were really tight, we might undertake it. But our sort of equipment isn't meant for winter, and there's no use risking colds when you'll have all the time you want next spring and summer. By the way, Sherman, did you send that letter to Mr. Grimstone?"

"Yes, sir. Ted and Ranny and I made it up, and all the fellows signed it. I posted it on Wednesday."

"That's good. I wrote him, myself, but I wanted him to see that you fellows, as well, appreciated what he's done." He rested his head against a tree-trunk and glanced appraisingly around the glade. "What a place this would be for a log-cabin!" he remarked.

"Immense!" exclaimed Court Parker, sitting suddenly upright. "With a big stone fireplace at one end."

"And bunks!" added Sanson, enthusiastically. "And shelves where we could keep pans and things. And–"

"We could camp here any time of the year then, couldn't we?"

"Sure! And think of coming in when your hands and feet are 'most frozen from skating, and thawing out before a roaring blaze, and making some cocoa,–oh, yum! Do you s'pose there's any chance, Mr. Curtis, of his letting us–" Sherman broke off with a sigh. "I forgot. He doesn't want any timber cut."

"No; and I'd scarcely like to ask him, anyway, after he's been so decent," said the scoutmaster. "It would look as if we didn't appreciate what he's done already." His glance swept thoughtfully around the open space again as if he were seeing in his mind's eye the structure that had excited such instant enthusiasm. "Of course, it would be quite possible to cut enough timber for a cabin without in the least hurting the woods; in fact a little thinning would do them good."

"Wouldn't it be a corking place to feed the birds from in winter!" suddenly spoke up Paul Trexler, a silent, reserved sort of chap. "We started up three or four covies of quail between the road and here."

"It certainly would!" The scoutmaster's tone was emphatic. "You've hit the best argument in its favor yet, Paul. The woods are fairly teeming with birds of all sorts; I noticed it as we came along. The place has been barred to the public for so long that I dare say the wild creatures have come to feel more or less safe here. With a cabin right on this spot we could keep grain in fairly large quantities, and when the heavy snows come, it would be easy to establish regular feeding-stations at different points, and–"

A sudden yelping made him break off and turn quickly, to see a large dog burst from the thicket at one side of the glade. With hair bristling and teeth bared, the animal pulled up abruptly and started a furious barking.

The scouts leaped up and several snatched sticks from the woodpile. An instant later, however, the low, sweeping hemlock branches parted, and Caleb Grimstone himself stepped into the open. With a snarl he silenced the dog and sent him groveling to heel. Then he faced Mr. Curtis and the boys with an odd, embarrassed defiance that made the former suspect his appearance had not been intentional, but was rather the result of the dog's outburst.

"This is mighty nice, Mr. Grimstone!" exclaimed the scoutmaster, advancing with outstretched hand. "You see we haven't lost any time in taking advantage of your kindness."

"Huh!" mumbled the old man. "I was jest takin' a little walk, an' heard voices–"

He paused awkwardly, glowering around the circle of wide-eyed boys.

"I had no idea you were able to walk so far," put in Mr. Curtis, quickly, "or we'd certainly have invited you to eat lunch with us. Won't you let the boys cook you something now? They're mighty proud of the way they can–"

"I've had dinner," interrupted the old man, hastily. He fumbled for a moment with the stout cane he carried; then his gaze returned to the scoutmaster. "I heard you sayin' somethin' about feedin' birds," he said curtly. "I didn't know you– What was it you meant?"

Briefly Mr. Curtis explained their methods of establishing feeding-stations through the woods and caring for them. When he had finished, Mr. Grimstone nodded.

"Humph!" he commented grumpily, "I–I like the birds. One o' the reasons I wouldn't–" He paused again and glowered at the boys. "They couldn't make a log-cabin," he stated positively. "It would be too much like real work."

A sudden stir went through the group. Mr. Curtis smiled. "I should hate to set them at it unless I really wanted it done," he laughed.

"How'd they know what trees to cut an' what to leave? They'd make a mess o' the whole place."

"Not with proper supervision," argued Mr. Curtis.

"Would you look after it?" inquired the old man, sharply.

"Certainly! I'd gladly constitute myself general foreman."

"Humph!" There was a momentary pause, tense with suspense. A battery of eyes, eager, expectant, pleading, was turned upon the old man, whose bent shoulders straightened a bit. "Wal, you can go ahead, then," he agreed crustily. "But all I can say is–"

A quick exclamation from the scouts drowned the remainder of his words. "G–e–e!" came hissing from a score of lips in a long sigh of rapture. It was followed by a bedlam of excited chatter.

"The greatest thing I ever heard!" exploded Ted MacIlvaine, enthusiastically. "A log-cabin, fellows–think of it! A troop cabin!" With eyes shining, he stepped suddenly forward and faced the crowd. "Three cheers for Mr. Grimstone, fellows!" he cried; "and make 'em good ones!"

When the last echo had died away, a faint touch of pink tinged the old man's leathery brown skin. But his frown abated nothing of its fierceness as he turned to the scoutmaster.

"Tut-tut–nonsense!" he grumbled. "I'll leave it to you, then; you'll be responsible, mind! I s'pose you know what trees to take out–or you ought to. Nothin' over eight inches, remember, an' not a scrap o' rubbish left lyin' around when you're done."

Without waiting for a reply, he turned abruptly and stalked off, a lean, bent, shabby figure with a nose like an eagle's beak and fiercely beetling brows. To the boys staring after him he was an angel in disguise.

CHAPTER XI

ELKHORN CABIN

All that week the members of Troop Five could talk or think of little else save the wonderful log-cabin which was to arise like magic on the shore of Crystal Lake. That, at least, was the way many of them pictured it as going up, but at the meeting on Monday night Mr. Curtis gave a little talk in which he pointed out that the undertaking could only be carried through by a good deal of hard, persistent labor, which would undoubtedly grow more or less tiresome before the end was reached.

"Saturday is really the only day when we can all get together," he said, "and there won't be many of them before the snow comes to put a stop to things. If we mean to enjoy it this winter, we've got to give every spare minute of our time to the work. There can't be any slowing down or backing out. Now, if you'd rather wait till spring, when we can take things more easily–"

"No, sir!" came in a swift, united chorus of protest. "We want to start now. We want to have it this winter."

The scoutmaster smiled a little. "That's the way I feel myself," he said; "so we'll consider that part settled. We'll meet here, then, next Saturday morning at half past eight, prepared to put in a strenuous day. I'll tell the different patrol-leaders what tools are needed, and they can look them up during the week. There's another thing. We'll have to buy considerable material, such as cement, boards for the floor and roof, window- and door-casings, and the like. That money should be earned by the troop, and I think it would be a good plan for Ward, MacIlvaine, and Phelps to meet at my house to-morrow afternoon or evening to discuss ways and means. Is that agreeable?"

It proved to be, when the question was put to vote and decided unanimously in the affirmative. The meeting ended with the enthusiasm over the project unchecked by this placing of it on a strictly methodical and businesslike basis.

That enthusiasm continued throughout the week, and when the crowd assembled on Saturday, Bennie Rhead, who was housed by a bad cold, was the only absentee. The others, laden with axes, saws, hatchets, an adz or two and some wide wood-chisels until they resembled a gang of pioneers, were in high spirits and eager to begin work. Their interest was heightened by the production of a plan Mr. Curtis had drawn up, showing a cabin twenty by sixteen feet, with a big stone fireplace opposite the door, two windows, and a double tier of bunks, one on each side of the entrance.

During the week the scoutmaster had gone over the ground with Mr. Grimstone and marked certain trees which were to be taken out, mainly white pines from six to eight inches in diameter that were too closely crowded to develop properly, so there was no delay in starting work. Immediately on reaching the point, the entire troop was divided into groups of three or four, each under the leadership of a boy who knew how to handle an ax. As soon as he felled a tree the others trimmed off the scanty limbs, sawed it into proper lengths, and stacked these up in piles on either side of the glade.

By noon the piles had assumed such proportions that after luncheon half of the wood-cutters were called off and set to notching the ends of the log, about eight inches from the end, and this was work in which everybody could take part. The notches were made on opposite sides of the log, about eight inches from the end, and were a quarter the thickness of the timber in depth. The logs averaged pretty much the same diameter, so that, when fitted together at right angles with the under notch on one side resting in the upper notch on the other, the whole length was snugly in contact, with scarcely any chinks to be filled in.

"That's the great advantage of pine," said Mr. Curtis, when he had explained the method to the boys. "Almost any hard wood will have bumps and twists in it, but the trunks of pines growing as thickly as these are practically straight from one end to the other."

"Are we going to build up the four walls solid, and then cut holes for the door and windows and fireplace?" asked Paul Trexler, who had evidently been reading up on the construction of cabins.

The scoutmaster shook his head. "That's the way many of them are made, but I could never quite see its advantage. It's a mean job, sawing the openings, and the full-length logs are lots harder to handle than shorter ones, to say nothing of the waste of timber. Of course there'll have to be full-length ones under and over the windows and over the door; but if we measure accurately, there's no reason why we shouldn't leave these openings as we go along, and so save time and labor. Spiking the door- and window-casings to the logs will hold them together firmly enough."

The cabin had already been staked out, and when, presently, the lower logs were set in place it was amazing what a difference the sight of that simple rectangle made. Instantly the visualizing of their dream became nearer and more concrete to the boys, its possibilities more apparent. They could see at a glance its size and shape and spaciousness. Entering through the door space, one could say that here would be the bunks, there the windows, and that gap opposite, the fireplace. It stimulated every one to renewed efforts. Blisters and tired muscles were forgotten in the eager desire to get another tier of logs into position. When Mr. Grimstone stalked into view, toward the middle of the afternoon, he was greeted by urgent invitations to "Come ahead and see how the cabin's going up!"

The old man responded stiffly, but it was impossible to maintain that attitude long in the face of the boisterous, whole-hearted enthusiasm of twenty boys. Inside of ten minutes he was chuckling over the awkward efforts of one scout to handle an adz and showing him the proper method. Within an hour, one would never have known him for the crusty, crabbed recluse who had been at odds with the Hillsgrove boys for more than a generation. He had shown the scouts a splendid place to get rocks for the fireplace, and told them how to make, with two poles and some cross saplings, a sort of litter for carrying the larger ones; he had made the rounds of the wood-choppers and watched them interestedly, criticizing, suggesting, and even cracking a dry joke or two at their expense. But his interest seemed to center in the building operations, to which he finally returned. When Mr. Curtis followed him a little later, he paused at the edge of the glade, a quiet smile curving his lips.

The old man stood amid a group of boys who were notching the logs. He had evidently been showing them some improvement on their methods, for as the scoutmaster stood there, he heard one of them say: "Is that right, Mr. Grimstone? Is that the way you mean?"

The old man nodded. "You've got it, son; you'll find that'll save you a lot of time."

"Say, Mr. Grimstone," piped up Harry Vedder, from the other side of the cabin, "won't you come over here, please?"

"You wait a minute, Dumpling!" admonished Bob Gibson. "I'm next. He promised to give me some points about fitting 'em together."

The scoutmaster's smile deepened as he came forward. "I guess I'll have to appoint you building foreman, Mr. Grimstone," he said. "Looks as if you knew a lot more about log-cabins than I ever will."

From force of habit the other frowned, but his eyes were twinkling. "I'd orter, I reckon," he returned. "I built enough of 'em when I was loggin' up state. If it wan't for this pesky arm–"

"That needn't interfere. You won't have to lift a finger. The boys are only too ready to work when they know how. Seriously, if you could oversee the building part, it would help us a lot. Then I could give all my time to getting out the logs, cleaning up, and looking after the chimney."

"I s'pose I can," observed the old man, briefly. "I ain't fit for much else jest now– an' the sooner you're done, the sooner the mess'll be cleared up."

So it was arranged, and the following Saturday found Mr. Grimstone promptly on the job. There was no question of his pleasure in the work, in spite of the occasional grumblings to which he gave vent in odd moments when he was not entirely lost in the novel occupation. To these the boys paid scant attention. They seemed to realize that they were merely superficial and really meant nothing, and from the first they got on admirably with the old man. They even joshed and joked with him, and before long he was retorting with sundry dry comments that sent them off into shouts of laughter.

Under his supervision the cabin grew apace. When the logs were all cut and carried in, Mr. Curtis devoted himself mainly to the stone chimney which, though necessarily slower and more difficult work, progressed very well. The opening was made to take four-foot logs, and the stone facing filled up more than half that end of the cabin. The boys could not wait for its completion to give it a baptism of fire. When the sides were up three feet or more, they kindled a blaze and cooked lunch there–the first meal to be prepared in the cabin.

Another celebration marked the setting of the ridge-pole; and when the roof was laid, it seemed as if the end was actually in sight. In the meantime, the important detail of earning money to pay for necessary materials had not been lost sight of. It had been decided that the scouts should go about this either singly or in groups, as they preferred. A number of suggestions were made by Mr. Curtis, but it was impressed upon the troop that there must be no appeal for either work or money in any way that would in the least savor of begging.

Whatever they did must be real work, the sort that people wanted done whether or not a scout cabin was in process of erection; and they must always give value received.

The methods resorted to seemed endless. Three boys who were adept with saw, hammer, and plane undertook the building of bird-houses, and their products were so well made and attractive that they had a hard time filling orders. Others raked up lawns, tended furnaces, cleaned cellars, sawed wood, and did a score of other varied chores. One entire patrol took up the subscription proposition of a big publishing-house and devoted themselves to it with such ardor that they cleared up nearly as much as all the rest together.

It can safely be said that few members of the troop had many spare minutes in the month that followed the starting of the cabin. There was no time for sports or games or reading stories. The public library was deserted. Of course there were a few who tired of the constant pressure and managed to escape a Saturday's labor by some flimsy pretext, but, on the whole, they stuck to it with remarkable perseverance. And when the last stone was in place on the chimney-top, the last chink filled, the last nail driven, there wasn't a boy in all that twenty-five who didn't feel a thrill of proud achievement at the result of their united efforts.

CHAPTER XII

A CRY IN THE NIGHT

Very seldom does reality come up to expectation, but this was one of the rare exceptions. It was the very cabin of their dreams that rose, a concrete fact, before their admiring gaze. As they stood off surveying the walls of neatly fitting logs, the sloping roof where a covering of split saplings concealed the useful, waterproof tar-paper, the square, workmanlike chimney rising beyond, there was a moment of almost awed silence, broken presently by Court Parker.

"Some cabin!" he exclaimed, voicing the feeling of them all. "It doesn't seem as if we could have built that ourselves, fellows."

"We did, though–we and Mr. Curtis and Mr. Grimstone!" jubilated Ted MacIlvaine. "Gee! Think of its being finished, and think of its being ours! Come on inside."

They went with a rush and broke into eager loud-voiced admiration of their handiwork. They tried the bunks, stout frameworks of pine with lengths of heavy canvas stretched tightly over them, and pronounced them better than any mattress, clamorously upheld the merit of one piece of work over another, and discussed the need of a table, chairs, and various other conveniences. Of course a fire was started, and when the red blaze roared up the chimney they rejoiced at the perfection of the draught. Then began a strenuous altercation as to what the cabin should be called which bade fair to end in a deadlock, owing to the wide variety of suggestions.

Neither the scoutmaster nor Mr. Grimstone took part in this. The former believed in letting the boys settle such questions unaided, while the old man so unaffectedly enjoyed the boys' delight that he simply sat in the background, silent, but with twinkling eyes. When a lull came in the dispute, however, he bethought himself of something.

"There's a pair of elk horns down to the barn you boys may as well have," he remarked. "You can hang 'em up over the fireplace for an ornament."

"Elk horns!" exclaimed Dale Tompkins. "They'd be dandy! Say!" he went on eagerly, stirred by sudden inspiration, "what's the matter with that for a name, fellows–Elkhorn Cabin?"

"Swell!" agreed two or three scouts at once. "That's better than any we've had. Sounds like the real thing, doesn't it?"

A vote was promptly taken, and though Ranny Phelps and a few others were against it, the majority approved. The horns, a fine pair of antlers, were fetched and hung in place, and the cabin formally christened.

"And next week," said Frank Sanson, as they were packing up for their tramp home through the crisp twilight, "we can come out to camp, can't we, Mr. Curtis?"

The scoutmaster nodded. "Provided the weather is decent and you all get your parents' consent, I don't see any reason why we shouldn't spent Friday night here. It may be a bit crowded, but we'll manage some way."

As a matter of fact they did not have to. Indeed, there came very near being no overnight hike at all. During the building of the cabin the weather had been singularly favorable. It was snapping cold much of the time but save for a flurry or two of snow, the days had been uniformly clear. Now, however, as if to make up for her smiles, Nature proceeded to frown. Wednesday was overcast, and all day Thursday a cold rain came down to damp the spirits of the would-be campers. It turned to snow during the night, and next morning found the country-side covered with a mantle of white. The temperature was well below freezing and dropping steadily, and Mr. Curtis, who had practically given up the idea of occupying the cabin that night, was surprised toward the middle of the afternoon by the appearance at his door of a group of white-flecked figures, very rosy of cheek and bright of eye, carrying blanket-rolls and hung about with cooking utensils and sundry parcels.

"We can go, can't we, sir?" inquired Ted MacIlvaine, eagerly, as he dusted the snow off his coat. "You're not going to give it up, are you?"

The scoutmaster's eyebrows lifted. "Have you all got permission?" he asked doubtfully.

"Yes, sir. We can go if you go," came in a prompt chorus.

For a moment Mr. Curtis hesitated. After all, there couldn't be any risk about the trip even if the storm continued all night. The cabin was weather-proof, and enough fire-wood had been cut to last them a week. With plenty of food and good blankets they would be as snug as possible, and he knew from experience the charm of the woods in a snow-storm. Looking the bunch over appraisingly, he saw that there were only seven–MacIlvaine, Parker, Dale Tompkins, Frank Sanson, Bob Gibson, Turk Gardner and Pete Oliver, all self-reliant boys of the type who were willing to stand a little roughing it without complaint.

"Are you the only ones who want to go?" he asked.

"Yes, sir," returned MacIlvaine. "Sherman's away, and Wes has a cold. The others all thought–"

"Cold feet!" stated Oliver, derisively, running his fingers through a thatch of bright, red hair. "They're afraid they might get a chill."

"Not much danger of that when you're around, Pete," laughed the scoutmaster. "Well, you boys had better come in and wait. It'll take me ten or fifteen minutes to get ready."

He appeared in rather less than that time, sweatered, mackinawed, with high, laced boots, woolen cap, and heavy gloves. Over one shoulder swung his blanket-roll, and strapped to his back was a good-sized haversack of provisions. He knew from experience that some one was sure to have forgotten something, so he always went prepared to supply deficiencies.

It was a joyous, hilarious bunch that made their way through the town and out along the Beldon Turnpike. Most of them had their staves, and two had brought snow-shoes along. Their attempts to use these unfamiliar articles occasioned much amusement among the others.

It took the better part of two hours to reach the cabin. The snow had drifted considerably, and the road was scarcely broken through. After they reached the woods the going was especially hard, and a general shout of rejoicing went up as the first sight of the sloping, snow-covered roof loomed up through the twilight. When the door was unlocked they entered with a rush, packs and blanket-rolls were dropped, and a fire started at once. When this was blazing merrily, Mr. Curtis divided the boys into two squads, one of which undertook preparations for supper and straightened up the cabin generally, while the others scraped a path through the snow down to the shore of the lake.

There were minor mishaps, of course, in the culinary department. A few chops were burned, and the baked potatoes resembled lumps of charcoal rather than things edible. But there was plenty for all, and nothing had ever tasted so good as the supper eaten there on the floor before the dancing flames. Afterward, when things were cleared away and the boys sprawled out on their blankets before the fireplace, the two lanterns were extinguished and only the red glow of the fire illumined the half-circle of eager young faces. The wailing of the wind in the pines and the soft, whispering beat of snow against the windows served only to intensify the cozy warmth and cheer of the cabin. Instinctively the boys drew closer together and, snuggling in their blankets, discussed for a space the unbelievable stupidity of any sane person preferring a humdrum evening at home to this. Then some one besought Mr. Curtis to tell a story.

"What kind of a story?" asked the scoutmaster, smiling.

"Oh, a ghost story, of course!" urged several voices at once.

Mr. Curtis laughed, stretched out his legs comfortably, thought for a minute or two, and then in a slow, sepulchral voice began a narrative which he called "The Headless Horseman of the Harlem." It was a tale full of creeps and thrills, abounding in dank vaults, weird apparitions, wild storms, midnight encounters, and various other appropriate settings and incidents. The boys drew closer still, luxuriating in the "spookiness" of it all, and then, just as some of the more impressionable were beginning to cast nervous glances behind them, he ended with a ridiculous climax that brought forth a shout of laughter and turned the whole thing into a farce.

A "round-robin" followed, the scoutmaster starting a yarn and leaving it at an exciting and dramatic moment for the boy on his right to continue. The absurdity of these continuations kept the crowd in a constant gale of merriment, and when the round was made they clamored for another. But it was growing late, so Mr. Curtis substituted a brief anecdote of scout bravery which had a humorous twist. It was the story, so often repeated in scout annals, of a little fellow plunging unhesitatingly to the rescue of a bigger boy who had stumbled beyond his depth in a swimming-hole. The stronger lad seized his rescuer about the neck and forced his head below the water. The youngster was unable to free himself, but with head down and breath almost gone, he hit bottom, and then, calmly walking along it, he tugged along his struggling friend until the bank was reached.

"He simply kept his head, you see, and used his brain, which is one of the best things scouting teaches us," concluded Mr. Curtis. He stood up, stretching. "Blankets out, fellows," he went on, "and everybody in bed."

Each bunk had been planned to accommodate two occupants, so there was no crowding or necessity for makeshifts. The fire was piled up with fresh logs, and though there was a good deal of preliminary laughter and chattering, the boys were too tired to stay awake long, even under the novel conditions. Bob Gibson was one of the last to close his eyes. He had the outside of one of the lower bunks with a full view of the fire, and though few would have suspected his gruff, matter-of-fact manner to overlay even a touch of poetry or imagination, he lay there watching it for a long time, fascinated by the leaping, dancing, crimson-yellow flames, until sleep at length overtook him.

How long he lay oblivious to sights and sounds he had no idea. But it must have been hours later when he found himself sitting bolt upright, every nerve tingling and in his ears the echo of that strange, horrible cry that had shocked him into complete wakefulness.

"What's that?" came in a tense, frightened gasp from one of the boys across the room.

Bob did not answer. He sat there shaking nervously and straining his ears for a repetition of the ghastly sound. The fire had died down to a bed of dull red embers, and there was a noticeable chill over everything. He caught his breath as a dark shadow swiftly passed him and then realized, with a feeling of keen relief, that it was Mr. Curtis. A moment later the scoutmaster had thrown an armful of light wood on the embers and the fire blazed up, illumining the pale faces of the boys, strained, startled, but all tense with expectation.

Suddenly the cry came again, a piercing, strangled, high-pitched scream that turned the blood cold and brought out beads of perspiration on more than one forehead. It seemed to come from just outside the cabin door.

CHAPTER XIII

WHAT THEY FOUND

By this time MacIlvaine and Frank Sanson had tumbled out of their bunks, and Bob followed their example.

"Wha–what is it, sir?" he asked, striving to keep his voice steady.

"I don't know," returned Mr. Curtis, briefly. He had slid into his riding-breeches and was hurriedly dragging on the heavy boots. "That's what we'll have to find out."

Bob hastily caught up his trousers. "It–it sounded like somebody being–choked," he said shakily.

Every one was out on the floor now, grabbing hastily for his clothes. Oliver caused a momentary spasm of mirth by trying to crowd both feet into one trouser-leg, but for the most part the boys huddled on their things in silence, shivering a bit from cold and nervousness. In about two minutes they were ready, and, catching up their staves, they hurried out into the open, the scoutmaster leading the way.

It had stopped snowing, and overhead a few stars gleamed coldly out of the blue-black sky. The wind had died down and the snow-clad woods stretched away before them, dim, white, oppressively silent, the tree-trunks black, the laden hemlocks distorted into queer shapes and shadows.

The bright gleam from the scoutmaster's flash-light, sweeping the snow about the cabin door, showed it unbroken by a single footprint of man or animal. They pushed on through the group of hemlocks, showering themselves with icy particles, but still they neither saw nor heard anything unusual. Then, just as some of the sounder sleepers were beginning to wonder whether they might not have dreamed it all, there rang out suddenly from among the tall laurel-bushes to their left a piercing, gurgling scream.

The horrible sound, so much clearer and more blood-curdling in the open, seemed to paralyze them all. For a fraction of a second they stood motionless; then Mr. Curtis plunged forward through the snow, and the rest followed in a straggling group, eyes starting and hands spasmodically clenching their staves.

"It's somebody being–murdered!" gasped Bob Gibson, huskily. "I knew the minute I heard it that something awful–"

He broke off with a queer, inarticulate murmur. Mr. Curtis had stopped so suddenly that the boy just behind narrowly escaped running into him. Throwing back his head, he sent peal after peal of laughter ringing through the silent woods. The scouts stared, dazed, as if they thought he had taken leave of his senses.

"What is it, sir?" begged two or three voices at once. "What–"

The scoutmaster choked and gurgled speechlessly, waving one arm helplessly toward the woods ahead. Several of the keenest-eyed thought they saw a vague, dark shadow moving silently across the snow; but it meant nothing to them, and they turned back to their leader, as bewildered as before.

"What a sell!" gasped the latter, striving to regain his self-control; "what an awful sell!" He succeeded in choking down his laughter, but there were tears of mirth in his eyes as they swept the staring circle. "It's nothing but an owl, fellows," he chuckled.

"An owl!" exclaimed Ted MacIlvaine, incredulously. "An owl–making a noise like that!"

The scoutmaster nodded and wiped his eyes. "An owl," he repeated. "There! Listen!"

To-whoo-hoo-hoo, to-whoo-whoo. A full, deep-toned note, like the distant baying of a hound, was wafted back through the woods. The strained expression on several faces relaxed, but they still looked puzzled.

"That's more familiar," smiled Mr. Curtis. "It's a great horned owl. You look as if you didn't believe it yet, Bob," he added, "but that's what it is, all the same. I've never heard it give that other sound, but I ought to have known–" He broke off, chuckling. "He certainly gave us a shock! I suppose we'll never hear the end of it. Let's get back to the fire; it's sort of chilly here."

They lost no time in following the suggestion. Back in the cabin they fed the blaze with fresh wood, and, sleep being out of the question for a while, gathered close around it, giggling and chattering and laughingly comparing their emotions on awakening to that blood-curdling scream coming out of the night.

"I was scart stiff," frankly confessed Court Parker.

"Same here," echoed several voices.

But Bob Gibson declined to treat the incident with the careless levity of the others. "I'd like to shoot the beast!" he growled vindictively, thinking of the way his nerves and feelings had been played upon.

"It would be the best thing that could happen," put in Mr. Curtis, decidedly. "We'll have to see if we can't manage it. Most owls are not only harmless, but a real benefit, living as they do mainly on rats and mice. But this creature can do more damage than any other bird except one or two species of hawks. A single one of them will destroy whole covies of quail, kill partridges, ducks, and song-birds, to say nothing of all sorts of domestic fowls. I'll have to bring out a shotgun and see if I can't pot him, or there won't be any birds left for us to feed."

He made several trips to the neighborhood of the cabin during the following ten days, but it was not until the week after Christmas that he got sight of the big marauder and with a fine shot brought him down from the top of a tall hemlock. Several of the scouts who were with him rushed forward to secure the bird, and were surprised at the size of the buff-and-white body, with its great spread of wing, fierce, hooked beak, and prominent ear-tufts.

"We ought to have him stuffed," said Frank Sanson, holding it up at full length. "He'd certainly make a dandy trophy for the cabin."

Mr. Curtis agreed to undertake it, and that night sent the bird to a taxidermist in the city. It came back several weeks later, mounted in the most lifelike manner, and became one of the principal decorations of the cabin. Court at once christened it "Bob's alarm-clock," much to the mystification of the fellows who had not been present on that memorable night. They knew that something unusual had happened, but were never able to find out just what, for the "advance-guard," as the seven called themselves, kept the incident carefully to themselves, and Mr. Curtis never told.

Long before this an ample supply of grain had been taken out to their headquarters and several feeding-stations established in different parts of the woods. These consisted mainly of rough shelters made of saplings, hemlock boughs, or stacks of old corn-stalks, furnished by Mr. Grimstone, in which the grain was scattered. There could be no question of their value, for from the first the snow about them was covered with bird-tracks of every variety. Before long, too, scouts visiting these stations to replenish the supply reported that the birds were growing noticeably tamer. Instead of flying off at the first sight of the boys, they sat in the trees and bushes around the shelters with an air almost of expectancy. Later they took to swooping down on the grain the moment it was poured out, without waiting for the scouts to move away. The climax came when one day Dale Tompkins excitedly reported that: "A chickadee came and lit right on the bag to-day, sir. He didn't seem a bit afraid, and only hopped off when I began to scatter the grain."

"They'll do more than that if you treat them right," returned the scoutmaster. "I've known of several cases where not only chickadees, but wrens and juncos and snow-sparrows and even wilder birds have grown so fearless that they've fed readily from the hand. Why don't you fellows try it? The main thing is to get them used to your bringing food to a certain place, and, when they're about, not to make any sudden movement that might frighten them. It would be rather fun to see how many varieties you could tame."

The idea met with general favor and when put into practice was remarkably successful. There also developed not a little good-natured rivalry among the boys as to which would first report the presence of a new bird at the feeding-stations; all of which helped to keep up the interest in the work and prevent it becoming monotonous and tiresome.

CHAPTER XIV

THE BOY WHO COULDN'T SWIM

The usual January thaw carried away most of the snow and made things generally sloppy and unpleasant. But it was followed by another cold snap, which put a glassy surface on the lake and drew the boys thither in greater numbers than ever. Almost every afternoon as soon as school was out a crowd of scouts, with skates slung about their necks and hockey-sticks in hand, might have been seen hurrying along the turnpike. Those who owned wheels made use of them; the others rode "shanks' mare," skylarking as they went and hilariously seizing every chance of a lift that came along.

Nor were they all members of Troop Five by any means. Mr. Grimstone had needed very little persuasion to grant the privileges of the lake to Hillsgrove scouts generally, and many were the exciting games of hockey that enlivened the winter afternoons. More often than not the clear, cold ring of steel on ice, the grate of swiftly turning runners, the sharp crack of wood against wood, the excited shouts and yells of shrill young voices, resounded on the lake until the gathering twilight made it difficult to distinguish one swiftly moving figure from another.

From its rocky elevation the log-cabin overlooked the active scene, smoke rising from its hospitable chimney and the red glow of a blazing fire gleaming in the windows and winking through the often opened door. Here congregated those who were too indifferent or unskilful to indulge in hockey, while every now and then a player would dash in to thaw out. On Fridays there was pretty sure to be a crowd spending the night there, and then the odor of crisping bacon or broiling chops mingled with the fragrance of the pines; the laughter and joshing kept up throughout the evening, and from the gray farmhouse across the lake an old man, glimpsing the cheery yellow gleam, would chuckle to himself and rub his knotted hands softly together.

"Them boys are havin' a good time ag'in to-night," he would murmur. "Reckon I'll hev' to step over an' see 'em in the mornin'."

Whenever he appeared he was sure of a hearty welcome, for underneath that crustiness, caused by years of loneliness and narrow living, the scouts had found a spirit as young and simple and likable, almost, as a boy's. And the old man, reveling in this novel, pleasant intercourse, felt sometimes as if he were beginning life all over again.

In this wise the winter passed with its usual mingling of work and play. Coasting, hockey, snow hikes, and the like mixed healthfully with regular lessons, the bird-feeding, studying up for merit badges or first- or second-class tests, and other scout duties and activities. The skating, particularly, was unusually prolonged, and the first signs of March thaws met with general regret.

"Well, we can have one more good game, anyhow," remarked Frank Sanson, as they came out of school at noon. "Maybe it will be a little soft, but it will bear all right. Who's going out?"

There were a number of affirmative replies, though the general opinion seemed to be that the ice would be too sloppy to have much fun.

"I'm going to try it, anyhow," Frank declared, as he got on his wheel. "See you fellows out there."

"Don't take any chances before we come," Sherman Ward called after him. "Remember you can't swim."

Sanson sniffed and shouted back a hasty denial of the charge. Nevertheless, as he rode home for dinner he was glad the time was coming when no one would be able even to hint at his deficiencies in that line. When it came to taking care of themselves in the water the boys of Hillsgrove had been more or less handicapped in the past, and like a number of others, Frank could swim only a few strokes. This spring, however, with the lake at his disposal, he meant to devote every spare minute to gaining proficiency in the art, so that when the time came for their summer camp he need ask no odds from anybody.

He finished dinner early and, with skates and hockey-stick, rode briskly out to the lake. He expected to be the first one there, but on the wood-road he noticed the fresh tracks of another bicycle, and, reaching the cabin, he found Paul Trexler standing before the fireplace, in which a lively blaze was going.

"Gee! You couldn't have had much dinner," he remarked.

"I brought it with me," exclaimed the boy, who was a rather silent lad with an unusual capacity for enjoying his own company. "Anybody else coming out?"

"Sure; quite a bunch. Tried the ice yet?"

"No; I was just going to."

"Come ahead, then," urged Sanson, briskly. "It'll be about our last chance, and I don't want to lose any time."

They put on their skates at the edge of the lake and then tested the ice. It was noticeably soft, especially near the shore, but seemed firm enough. Farther out it was better, and as they skated up and down together Frank decided that they would have their game even if they did get pretty wet before it was over.

"Guess I'll go up a ways and sort of explore a little," said Trexler, presently. It was almost his first remark since leaving the cabin, and his tone did not indicate any special desire for company.

"All right," nodded Sanson. "Go ahead, only be careful about the ice. Mr. Grimstone says there are springs up there, and you know this is just the weather to make them dangerous." For a moment or two he stood watching the thin, stooping figure sweeping up the lake; then he smiled. "He's a queer duck," he murmured. "I should think he'd get awful tired of just playing around with himself that way. Wish the others would hurry up."

There were no signs of them, however, so he set himself to master an intricate figure he had been trying for several days past. Though there were no swimming facilities about the village, the annual flooding and freezing over of a flat meadow on the outskirts gave the fellows a very decent chance for skating, of which most of them had availed themselves. Sanson was one of the most proficient in the sport and enjoyed it thoroughly, especially now that the spacious lake gave them so much greater scope. His runners cut the ice in sweeping, graceful curves, and each time the momentum carried him nearer to the completion of the figure. Once or twice he noticed Trexler up toward the outlet, but it was in a vague sort of way, with a mind concentrated on his own evolutions.

"It's coming all right," he said aloud, pausing for a second to get his breath. "I've got the hang of it now. One more try and I can make it."

But Fate willed otherwise. As a matter of fact, Frank did not make that final effort which was to bring him success. He skated over to a clear spot on the ice and was swinging along to get up speed when a sudden panicky cry from up the lake made him stop and whirl around with a grind of steel runners that threw up a shower of icy particles.

Trexler was nowhere to be seen! For a fraction of a second Frank stared open-mouthed at the bare expanse of ice narrowing to the outlet, spanned by the old stone bridge. Then his sweeping glance paused at a dark, irregular patch in the glistening surface where something seemed to move feebly, and with a smothered cry he dug his skates into the ice and sped up the lake.

The stick slid over the jagged edges of the hole

The distance was not really great, but to the frightened boy it seemed interminable. Almost at once he recognized the spot as open water in the midst of which Trexler's white face and clawing hands striving frantically for a hold on the treacherous, splintering edges stood out with horrible distinctness–Trexler, who could not swim a stroke!

Frank shuddered and dug his teeth into his under lip. For the matter of that, he himself was almost as helpless. With a sick, sinking pang it was borne in on him that the few halting strokes he had learned to take in smooth water last summer would be next to useless in an emergency like this. But he did not pause nor lessen his speed. He only knew that he could not hesitate, with that anguished face and those clutching hands to spur him on.

"Hold on a minute longer, Paul!" he cried, when he was within twenty feet of the hole. "Don't let go. I–I'll–get you out!"

Jerking at the lever of his skates, he kicked them off. The hockey-stick was still in his grasp, and, with this outstretched, he flung himself flat on the ice and wriggled forward. He paid no heed to the ominous cracking beneath him; there was no time for caution. Trexler had lost the slight grip he had had on the crumbling edges of the hole and was beating the water madly with his hands. His eyes, wild with despairing horror, were fixed on Frank with a desperate pleading that made the boy oblivious to everything save the vital need of haste.

With a sharp thrust of both feet, he pushed himself forward. The stick slid over the jagged edges of the hole and straight into the groping hands that closed over and hung upon it with the tenacious grip that knows no reason.

"Don't jerk it!" cried Sanson, sharply, as the ice creaked and cracked beneath him. "Just hold tight and let me draw you in."

But Trexler was too far gone to heed. There came another crack more ominous than the others. Even now, by letting go the stick, Frank could have escaped by rolling swiftly to one side or the other. He wanted to–desperately; but something within him stronger even than his fear clenched his fingers around the tape-wound hickory.

In another second the ice on which he lay gave with a crash and plunged him into the icy water.

CHAPTER XV

THE RESCUE

As he went under, Sanson's first feeling was one of utter panic. The shock and cold, above all the horrible sense of suffocation, started him struggling as madly and ineffectually as Trexler had done a moment before. Then all at once, out of the whirling turmoil of fear which filled his soul, some vague remembrance of the brief lessons last summer stood forth, and he thrust downward with his feet. The motion was almost entirely instinctive, but the result was curiously steadying. The moment that downward movement ceased, his brain seemed to clear and he got a grip on himself.

"I mustn't come up under the ice," he found himself thinking, as he pushed vigorously upward again.

Then his head cleaved the water and he gulped in the blessed air in long, deep breaths. An instant later this was cut off by the grip of arms about his neck as Trexler, whom he had momentarily forgotten, clutched at him with all the strength and determination of despair.

That there were approved methods of releasing such grips Frank knew from repeated perusals of the scout handbook, but not a vestige of them stuck in his mind now. Full of wild panic, he struck out blindly with all his power. Trexler's head went back under the impact; his grasp slackened. Sanson had a momentary glimpse of the white face with half-closed eyes and twisted lips all a-swirl with water, and again that impulse that was stronger than panic made him reach out and catch hold of the boy's shoulder. At almost the same instant something hard grazed his cheek, and he realized that the force of his blow had sent him against one side of the hole. With a grasp of thankfulness, he caught at it, finding the ice here fairly substantial. He drew Trexler's body closer to him, and for the first time since the plunge he had a moment in which to think.

"I mustn't try and climb out or it'll break," he muttered. "Why don't the fellows come? They must have got out by now." He quite failed to realize how short a space of time it was since he had first started to Trexler's aid. "I can't hold on here much longer. I'm freezing now, and–"

His voice broke a little, but he bit his lip and choked back the sob in his throat. Then, summoning all his strength, he tried to shout for help, but the result was a hoarse croak that could not have been heard a hundred feet away. To his utter astonishment it was answered from close at hand.

"Hold tight, Frank; we're coming!"

It was Sherman Ward's voice. Sanson could scarcely believe his senses, even though a moment later he heard the scrape of skates and the grating of a sudden stopping. It took him a moment or two to realize that he had become turned around and was facing the inlet and the bridge, so that the fellows had been able to approach from down the lake without his seeing them.

"Get that branch there," he heard Sherman order crisply. "Hustle! Can you keep up a bit longer, Frank?"

"S-s-sure!" answered Sanson, through chattering teeth. "Only be as qu-quick as you c-c-can. P-P-Paul–"

"We'll be there in half a shake. That's it, Dale. Shove it across. Now, you fellows hold fast to that end while I go out."

There was a scraping sound and the end of a stout branch appeared in front of Sanson. Then, more slowly, Sherman's head and shoulders came in sight as he crept cautiously out along it.

"I'll take him first," he said. "Can you raise him up a little?"

"I'm afraid not. My arm's all numb, and–"

"All right," interrupted the patrol-leader. "I'll manage. Hold fast back there."

He wriggled forward a bit more and, reaching down, managed to catch Trexler under the arms. To draw him out of the water was a more difficult business, but Sherman had good muscles and accomplished it without accident. The ice creaked and groaned, but evidently had not been much weakened by the treacherous spring, and it held. The arm with which Frank had been supporting the boy had absolutely no feeling in it, and the strain of gripping the slippery ice was growing unendurable. He shifted his hold to the stick, however, and a moment later he was half lifted, half helped out on the solid ice.

"Yours for the cabin, quick!" said Ward, tersely. "Here, Ted, give us a hand."

MacIlvaine stepped quickly forward, and together they hustled Sanson across the ice. At first, Frank could scarcely move his feet and had to be practically carried along. But gradually the rapid motion, the stumbling, recovering, and general jolting-up began to send the blood tingling back into his chilled body. Ahead of them he could see Ranleigh and Dale Tompkins supporting Trexler, and making even better speed than his own conductors. The sight of that limp body, with one hand dangling helplessly, brought to Frank a sudden stinging pang of remorse and apprehension as he remembered the frenzied blow he had struck the fellow.

"Paul–" he gasped; "is he–"

"It's the cold and shock mostly, I think," answered Sherman. "He's all in, but not really unconscious. Did he go down?"

"I don't think so. Not more than once, anyway."

There was no more conversation until after they reached the cabin. Frank was able to stumble up the rocky slope unaided, and, once inside, his clothes were stripped off and he was rolled in blankets that had been heated before the roaring blaze. Muffled in these, with some of the boys deftly rubbing his legs and arms, it wasn't long before a delicious languor crept over him and he actually felt like dozing off to sleep.

He might have yielded to the impulse but for his anxiety about Trexler. Paul lay in the opposite bunk and was being subjected to the same treatment as Frank, but he did not seem to be responding as readily as the more robust fellow. Of course, he had been longer exposed to the cold and shock, but Sanson did not think of that. He was still worrying over the ruthless manner in which he had struck the boy, and fearful that in some way the blow might be responsible for Trexler's condition. When Mr. Curtis and the doctor appeared, summoned by one of the fellows who had ridden hastily back to town on his wheel, Frank watched them apprehensively. When the scoutmaster at length came over to his bunk he sat up abruptly and poured forth his doubts and fears before the older man had time to say a word.

Mr. Curtis listened quietly, and when the boy had finished he smiled reassuringly and shook his head. "You needn't worry about that, Frank," he said. "The doctor says he'll come around all right. He's pretty well done up from the exposure and shock, and you know he's never been so very strong. I don't think your hitting him has had much to do with it, but even if it had, no one could blame you. It was a question of that, or of both of you going down, and in such an emergency almost any methods are right. How are you feeling yourself?"

"Oh, I'm all right now, sir. There's nothing at all the matter with me. I don't see why I can't get up."

"Better not just yet. There's nothing special you can do. I have a car over by the bridge, and when Paul is fit to be moved, we'll all go back together."

"But I've got my wheel here," protested Frank.

"Let somebody else ride it in," returned Mr. Curtis. "After such a dousing there's no use taking chances." He paused a moment, his eyes fixed quizzically on the boy's face. "You can't swim, can you, Frank?" he went on presently.

"Oh, yes, sir!" the boy said hastily.

A faint smile curved the man's lips. "How much?" he asked quietly. "About six strokes?"

Sanson flushed, and a guilty grin overspread his face. "Make it eight, sir," he chuckled. "A fellow can't seem to fool you at all."

"And yet you went in after–"

"But I didn't!" interrupted Frank, earnestly. "I was reaching out with my hockey-stick, and the ice broke and dropped me in. I didn't mean to at all."

"Broke without any warning, I suppose," murmured Mr. Curtis. "You couldn't possibly have escaped–even by letting go your stick."

The boy's flush deepened, and he wriggled uncomfortably. "I–I–" he stammered, and then was silent.

The scoutmaster gave a low, contented laugh, and something in his glance sent an odd thrill through Sanson. He didn't analyze it. He only knew that all at once he had ceased to feel embarrassed and was happy and comfortable, and back of it all not a little proud of the thing which had won his scoutmaster's commendation.

"I won't bother you any more," smiled Mr. Curtis, as he turned away. "I had an idea that was about how it happened, though."

A pleasant glow crept over the boy, continuing even after he had got into his clothes and was making his way along the shore toward the bridge. It was still present to a certain extent next day, and, combined with a touch of remorse that lingered in the back of his mind, brought him in the afternoon to the Trexler house to inquire for Paul, who had not appeared at school. He did not expect to see the boy, and when Mrs. Trexler asked him to come in, he was seized with a mild sort of panic.

"I was afraid of a cold, so I kept him home to-day. I know he'll want to see you," she said as Frank stepped into the hall and closed the door reluctantly behind him. "I want to–"

She broke off abruptly, and Frank, flashing a single startled glance at her, saw that her eyes were full of tears. Instantly he dropped his own and stood awkwardly twisting his cap and wishing he hadn't come.

"I know boys hate being thanked," Mrs. Trexler went on presently in a voice which wasn't quite steady, "so I won't pester you with–with a mother's gratitude. I just want you to let me–"

She bent over suddenly and kissed him on the forehead. The boy flushed crimson and mumbled something about its being only what any fellow would have done. Would Paul go on this way, too, he wondered apprehensively as he followed her down the hall. He supposed it was natural for a woman to get all worked up, but if a fellow–

"Some one to see you, Paul," said Mrs. Trexler, cheerfully, pausing beside an open doorway.

She motioned for Frank to enter and then, to his relief, departed, leaving the two boys alone. Paul had been reading beside a window, but as Sanson appeared he stood up slowly. Though looking much better than he had the afternoon before, his face was still a little pale, and the visitor perceived, with a sudden sense of returning composure, that he, too, was overcome with embarrassment. Somehow the discovery made things a lot easier.

"I–I'm awfully glad you came in," Trexler stammered. He put out his hand awkwardly, but there was a vigor in his lingering grip that told something of the feelings words refused to express.

"You–weren't in school, so I thought maybe you were–sick, or something," Sanson returned. "Gee! What a dandy room!"

Now that the worst was over he began to be rather glad he had come, and stared about him with eager interest. Certainly it was a room to excite any boy's enthusiasm. Long and rather narrow, there were two windows on one side through which the winter sun poured cheerfully. Against the opposite wall, and filling almost the entire space, was a large glass-fronted case, containing the most amazingly realistic reproduction of woodland life the boy had ever seen.

Fastened in one corner was the gnarled crotch of a tree with a great, roughly built nest of twigs and leaves from which two baby hawks, their down just giving place to feathers, thrust up inquiring heads. At the other end of the case stood a section of a silvery white oak, with one long branch extending along the back. An owl perched here, teased by a blackbird with outstretched wings and open beak, and there were several birds'-nests among the branches. The lower part of the case was filled with small bushes, clumps of grass, and reeds, among which Frank noted quantities of other nests, some with eggs and some without, more mounted birds of various sorts, and several animals, such as a mink, two squirrels, and a skunk, all in the most lifelike attitudes. Turning from an eager inspection of the case, he stared at Trexler in amazement.

"It's the greatest thing I ever saw!" he exclaimed. "Do you mean to say you did it all yourself?"

Paul nodded, his pale face tinged with color, his eyes sparkling. "It isn't hard when you know how to stuff things," he said. "I took lessons in the city before we came out here last year. It's been lots of fun fixing them up."

"But how the deuce did you get 'em all?" Frank turned quickly back to the case again. "You must be a dandy shot."

"But I'm not! I hate to kill things–especially birds. You see, I go off for long tramps a lot, and in the winter especially you often find birds that have been frozen, or killed by flying into things. Some of them people gave me. A farmer that I know out near Alton shot that skunk and the mink in his chicken-yard. The quail and that woodcock came from down South. A cousin of mine sent them up, and I got Mother to let me take the skins off before she cooked them."

"How about the hawks–those are hawks, aren't they?"

"Sure. Red-shouldered hawks. I s'pose I oughtn't to have taken them, but I wanted to try taming some. I knew where there was a nest, and last spring I got up the tree with climbers and took two. They were awful funny the way they'd sit up and cry whenever they saw me coming. I guess I must have fed 'em too much, or something, for they died in about a week. I won't try it again, you bet!"

Paul looked rather sheepish as he made this confession, and hurried on to another subject. "It's the same way about the eggs. I used to take only one out of a nest, but Mr. Curtis said even that was pretty hard on the birds, so I stopped. I haven't taken any since I've been a scout. It's more fun, really, taking pictures."

"Pictures of birds' eggs?"

"Oh, eggs and nests and birds–anything wild. It's dandy sport. I've got quite a lot of good ones if you'd like to see them."

Frank quickly acquiesced, and as Paul went over to a desk for the photograph book, his eyes followed the boy with an odd expression in them. Hitherto he had regarded Trexler with a certain measure of tolerance as a queer, unsociable sort of fellow, who seldom took part in the sports and pastimes of the troop, but preferred moping by himself. It had never occurred to him that the solitary rambles could be productive of anything like the results he saw about him. As he glanced again at the case, a dawning respect began to fill him for the boy who could do all this and yet remain so modest that not a whisper of it leaked out among his companions.

That respect deepened as Frank turned the pages of the album and examined scores of photographs of feathered wild things. There were not alone pictures of the commoner birds, but many of the shyer sort, like the cardinal, the oven-bird, and several varieties of thrush which rarely emerge from the deep woodland, and they had been taken in all sorts of positions. Trexler had even succeeded in getting a very good photograph of the great blue heron, and his account of the difficulties of that enterprise filled Sanson with enthusiasm.

"It must be great!" he exclaimed eagerly. "I wish I could go along with you some time and see how you do it."

"Why don't you? I'd like to have you–awfully."

There could be no mistaking the earnestness of the invitation, and Frank took it up promptly.

"All right; that's a go. You let me know the next time you go out, and I'll be there like a runaway freight-train." He rose to go, for to his surprise it was growing dark; he had no idea he had stayed so long. "You've certainly got a corking place here," he said, glancing around for the last time. "Why, you ought to be able to rake in a whole lot of merit badges. There's taxidermy and bird study and–"

"I'm only a second-class scout," interrupted Trexler, briefly. He flushed a little and twisted his fingers together. "You see, I–can't swim. But I'm going to learn," he added determinedly. "I'm going to start in the minute the water's warm enough and keep it up till I get the hang of it, even if it takes all summer."

"Same here," laughed Frank, as they reached the front door. "We'll be two dubs together, won't we? Good-by, and thanks for showing me all the stuff."

Out in the street he thrust both hands deep in his pockets and started briskly homeward, whistling. Presently he stopped and laughed rather sheepishly.

"Gee!" he muttered. "It's funny how you can get a fellow's number wrong–it sure is!"

CHAPTER XVI

TREXLER'S TRANSFORMATION

Sanson's account of his visit to Paul Trexler was received at first with a good deal of incredulity. But when he persisted that he wasn't trying to play any trick general curiosity was aroused among the fellows, and they began to drop in at the Trexler house to see for themselves the wonderful case of birds and the even more wonderful photographs. Before he knew it Paul became almost a public character.

At first he did not like it at all. Excessively shy by nature, he had gone his solitary way for so long that he didn't know how to take the jokes and banter and mild horse-play of a crowd of boys. But gradually he grew accustomed to it, and when he found that the fellows weren't making fun of him, as he at first supposed, but really regarded him with a marked respect for his unusual talents, he began actually to enjoy the situation.

He came to know the boys better, to find pleasure in their companionship. He no longer went off on those solitary tramps, for there was always some one ready and eager to accompany him. And little by little even these excursions began to grow slightly less frequent as he discovered, with a mild surprise, that there was a good deal of fun to be extracted from the regular sports and games and doings of the crowd.

Frank Sanson was mainly responsible for this. Keen, eager, full of enthusiasm about everything, he flung himself into all the school and troop activities with a zest which made him one of the livest boys in Hillsgrove. He could enjoy an occasional tramp in the woods with Trexler because of the novelty and interest of their search; but he could not understand any one wanting to devote himself exclusively to such an occupation.

"You miss half your life in not going more with the fellows, Paul," he remarked one day in early April. "Why don't you leave the old camera at home and come on up to the ball-field with me? We're going to have a great old practice to-day."

"But I can't play baseball," protested Trexler.

"Shucks! How do you know? Did you ever try?"

"N-o, but–"

"It's time you started in, then," interrupted Sanson. "Of course you can't expect to make the team this year, but you'll have a lot of fun playing with the scrub. Hustle up or we'll be late."

So Trexler went, mainly because he didn't exactly know how to refuse the boy he had come to like so much. But it was with a good deal of inward trepidation that he trailed after Frank to where Ranny Phelps, who captained the team, was chatting with Mr. Curtis's younger brother, just home for the Easter holidays. He had a feeling that he was going to make an awful exhibition of himself, and that conviction was not lessened by the slight lifting of the eyebrows with which Ranny greeted Frank's request that his friend be allowed to practise with the others.

But out in the field, nervously adjusting a borrowed glove, Paul was conscious of an odd, tingling sensation altogether different from apprehension. The day was typically April and fairly breathed of spring. Birds darted hither and thither, singing joyously. Beyond the low stone wall at one side the feathery outlines of a wild cherry, pale green, with touches of white blossoms just bursting into bloom, was etched against the sky in delicate tracery. Farther still, a man was plowing, and from the long straight furrows came that moist, fresh, homely smell of newly turned earth that one gets only in springtime. Out of the deep blue sky, flecked with fluffy, idly drifting clouds, the sun shone warm and caressing. From all about came the sound of quick, clear, eager voices, to which was presently added the crack of leather meeting wood, the thud of feet drumming the turf, and the duller sound of leather pounding against leather.

There was something about it all that stirred the boy and sent the blood running like quick-silver through his veins, yet which made him feel curiously alone and out of it. Other springs had meant to him the beautiful awakening of nature, the return of the birds he loved, the charm of wood and stream and open country-side at its best. But somehow that failed to satisfy him as it had in the past. Vaguely he felt that something was missing, he could not say just what. A feeling of emulation stirred him, a desire to take his part in the clash and struggle and ceaseless competition from which, till now, he had held aloof. Admiringly, with a faint touch of envy, he watched Frank Sanson make a difficult one-hand stop with seeming ease. Why hadn't he come out before and learned the game and how to uphold his end with the others? Was it too late even now? he wondered.

"Hi, Paul! Get under this one!"

The shout from Sanson roused Trexler to the realization that a fly was coming in his direction. He ran back a little, then forward. The ball seemed to be dropping with the speed of a cannon-shot, but he forced himself to meet it without shrinking. Thrusting up his hands awkwardly, he staggered a bit under its momentum, as he caught at it, and a burning sting tingled in the bare palm which had taken most of the impact. The ball, bouncing off, rolled to one side, and a laugh went round the field as he chased after it and threw it in. When he returned to his place Paul's face was crimson, but his lips were set in a stubborn line and he scarcely noticed the pain in his hand.

"I will get the hang of it!" he muttered under his breath. "I'll learn to do it right if–if it takes all season!"

He stuck to his position as long as any of the others, and on the way home, with some embarrassment, he spoke to Frank of his determination. The latter was delighted and offered to help him in any way he could. As a result, from that time forth the two rarely went anywhere without a baseball. Whenever there were a few minutes to spare they used them for throwing and catching. On the field, before and after the regular work, Frank knocked out flies or grounders, and in many other ways did his best to give his friend as much as possible of the practice he needed.

A baseball player isn't easily made to order. The normal boy seems almost to absorb his knowledge of the game through the pores of his skin, gaining proficiency by constant, never-ending practice that usually begins as soon as he is big enough to throw a ball. But much can be done by dogged persistence, and Paul Trexler had that quality to a marked degree. As the days passed, dust began to gather on his camera and on the cover of his book of bird photographs. In this new and strenuous occupation he found little time for the things which had formally absorbed him. He regretted the many long tramps he had planned, but somehow he failed to miss them as much as he expected. Each noticeable improvement in his game filled him with a deep, abiding satisfaction, surpassing even the delight which he used to feel on securing a fine photograph. The climax came that afternoon when he was allowed to play on the scrub in place of one of the fielders who had not shown up. Not only did he fail to make any mirth-provoking blunders, but he even put through one play that brought forth a surprised, approving comment from Ranny Phelps himself.

"I don't know what you've been doing to him, Frank," the latter said to Sanson, who passed on the remark afterward. "I've never seen anybody improve the way he has. That catch wasn't anything wonderful, of course, but when he threw to third he used his head, which is more than a lot of fellows right here on the field ever think of doing."

The latter part of the speech, especially, was typical of the handsome Ranleigh. He ran the ball-team as he did a good many other things, reaching decisions more often through impulse and prejudice than from a mature judgment. There could be no question of his knowledge of the game or his ability as a pitcher. The latter was really extraordinary for a fellow of his age and experience, and this, perhaps, was what made him so intolerant of less gifted players. At all events, he had a little trick of sarcasm which did not endear him to those on whom it was exercised. Most fellows take the ordinary sort of "calling down," especially if it has been earned, with a fair amount of grace, but it rarely does any good to rub it in, as Ranny so often did.

"You'd think he was a little tin god on wheels the way he struts up and down, digging into the fellows in that uppish, sneering way," Court Parker heatedly remarked one afternoon late in the season. "You might think he never made any errors himself."

"I don't suppose he really means anything by it," returned Dale Tompkins, rather deprecatingly. For some time that day he had been watching Phelps and wondering rather wistfully whether Ranny was ever going to entirely forget that impulsive flare-up of his so many months ago. For a long time, to be sure, there had been few signs of active animosity from the blond chap. It would be well-nigh impossible for any boy to long maintain that excessive coldness toward a fellow with whom he was so often and so intimately thrown. Especially since the beginning of baseball practice there had been a good deal of intercourse between them, but always Dale was conscious of a deep reserve looming up between them like some invisible, insurmountable barrier. And there were times when he would have given the world to break that barrier down.

Parker sniffed. "Then why does he do it? It only gets the fellows raw without doing a scrap of good. You're a great one to stand up for him, Tommy! He's treated you mean as dirt. Didn't he promise to let you pitch in some of the games?"

"Why, n-o; it wasn't exactly a promise."

"It was the same thing. He made you think he was going to put you in, and all spring you've worked your arm nearly off, pitching to the bunch. Then when a regular game came along he stepped into the box himself and hogged the whole thing nine innings. It's been the same ever since, except last week when you went in for one miserable inning after we'd won the game. I call that a–a–an insult. It looked as if he thought you weren't any good."

Dale shrugged his shoulders. "Maybe he does," he returned quietly. "He's a lot better pitcher than I am."

"Is he? Humph! He's nowhere near as steady, let me tell you. Wait till he gets up against a real team, and I shouldn't wonder a bit if he blew up. He did last year, and we mighty near lost the series. He can't stand being joshed, and Troop One is just the bunch to do it."

Dale laughed a little and set down his companion's disparaging remarks to temper rather than to any real belief in what he was saying. He had never seen Ranny pitch before this season, but he could not imagine him losing his superb control and "blowing up." He would have given anything for a chance to pitch against Troop One, but he had long ago given up hoping, Ranny made it only too clear that he meant to keep that honor for himself, just as he had monopolized the pitching in all the other games. Dale couldn't quite make up his mind whether this was from a deliberate desire to shut him out, or because the team captain really lacked faith in his ability and was afraid to trust him. Feeling as he did toward the other–liking, admiring him still, almost in spite of himself, Tompkins rather hoped it was the latter case. In either event, however, he was obliged to content himself with the cold comfort that with Ranleigh Phelps pitching his best Troop Five was practically certain to win.

The inter-troop baseball series had been arranged so that the two strongest teams were matched together on the concluding day. Both had won every game they had played so far, and the result this Saturday afternoon would decide the championship.

Naturally there was a big crowd of spectators. Practically every boy in town was present, ready to root for his favorite team, and the grand stand was well filled with older enthusiasts.

When Troop Five won the toss and spread out on the field, Dale Tompkins, with a faint sigh, dropped down on the bench he had ornamented for most of the season. Watching Ranny Phelps walking out to the mound, a wave of envy, pure and simple, swept over him. He wanted to pitch–desperately. At that moment he would have welcomed almost any contingency–even the unthinkable "blowing up" that Court had predicted–that would give him his chance. He had done practically nothing all the season, and it seemed unfair that the last game should come without giving him a single opportunity of showing his mettle.

"What's the use of trying at all if you never get a show?" he thought disconsolately.

But the mood did not last long. Dale was too keen a baseball fan not to become swiftly absorbed in the game which meant so much to himself and his brother scouts. There could be no question of Ranny's fine form. For the first five innings not a hit was scored against him. To be sure, several players made first on various errors, but none got beyond third, and in the meantime Troop Five had scored two runs.

"He's certainly some pitcher!" Tompkins remarked rather wistfully to Paul Trexler, who had taken a seat beside him. "Looks as if we had the game cinched."

"I hope so. If only he don't–er–blow up–"

"Blow up!" interrupted Tompkins, sharply. "Does he act like it? You've been listening to Court Parker's rubbish, Paul. I never saw any fellow pitch a steadier game."

But though he had been swift to deny the possibility, Trexler's remark lingered in Dale's mind, and almost unconsciously he began to watch for signs which might confirm it. The fellows that composed the rival team were rather older than the average scout and of a certain rough-and-ready type which made their joshing apt to carry more sting than that sort of thing usually does. So far, however, there had been little in the pitcher's manner or behavior for them to take hold of, and the stream of commonplace chatter and joking seemed to affect Ranny as little as water does a duck. He took it carelessly, with now and then an apt retort which turned the laugh against the other fellows, and throughout the sixth and seventh innings his work continued to show much of the smooth perfection it had displayed from the first.

It was in the beginning of the eighth that Tompkins's face began to grow a little troubled. Ranny had several rather noticeable mannerisms, which were especially apt to appear on the flood-tide of success. Whether deliberately or not, he had hitherto suppressed them, but now he seemed momentarily to relax his vigilance.

He had struck out the first batter, and as the second stepped up to face him the pitcher paused, swept the grand stand with a leisurely glance, and then tossed back his head in an odd, rather affected gesture before starting to wind up. The gesture had probably originated on the gridiron, where hair is worn rather long and is apt to trail into one's eyes; here it looked a bit foolish, and instantly one of the opposition, who was coaching at first base, a red-headed fellow named Conners, seized upon it.

"See him shake his mane, fellows!" he yelled in a shrill falsetto. "Don't let him scare you, Blakie; he's tame!"

"He'll be the goat, all right, before we get done with him," chimed in another.

Ranny hesitated an instant in his swing, bit his lips, and then put the ball over. It was wide, and, as he caught the return, there was an angry flush on his handsome face.

"Don't he blush sweetly?" shrilled Conners, dancing about off first. "He'd make a peach of a girl!"

Ranny wound up hastily and pitched again. It was a straight, speedy ball, but in his annoyance he must have forgotten that this was just the sort Blake liked. The latter met it squarely with a clean crack that brought Dale's heart into his mouth and jerked him to his feet to watch with tight lips and despairing eyes the soaring flight of the white sphere over the diamond and on–on–seemingly to the very limits of the outfield!

CHAPTER XVII

DALE'S CHANCE

To Tompkins, watching with bated breath and clenched fists, it seemed as if the ball would never drop. Two of the fielders were running swiftly backward, but there wasn't a chance in a hundred of their catching it. Bat flung aside and toe-clips digging into the ground, Blake was speeding toward first. Before the ball hit the turf he had rounded the sack. By the time Pete Oliver had recovered it and lined it in, the runner was panting on second.

"Got him going! Got him going!" shrieked Conners, delightedly. "Get after it, Peanut. Smash it on the nose and bring in Blakie!"

His team-mates added their jubilations to his, and a bedlam of shrill advice, mingled with fresh joshing, ensued. Ranny's eyes flashed with ill-concealed anger, and he gripped his under lip tight between his teeth. His first ball was good, but the batter fell on the second with all his might. Crack! A gasp went up from the watchers on the bench. Smack! The gasp merged into a yell of delight as the ball landed squarely in Frank Sanson's mitt and stuck there. The force of the impact nearly upset the short-stop, but he recovered swiftly and lined the horsehide straight into the outstretched hands of Court Parker, astride of third. There was a flashing downward motion of those hands, and the sliding runner was tagged, his fingers not six inches from the sack.

To the shout of delight that went up, Dale Tompkins contributed rather more than his share. Leaping and capering in front of the bench, it seemed as if he couldn't express his overwhelming relief at the unexpected ending of the inning and their escape from a dangerous situation. He thumped Sanson on the back and poked Court in the ribs joyously. But when the first excited enthusiasm had passed he began to think of the inning yet to be played and to wonder how Ranny would get through it. Surely there was time to pull himself together, the boy thought. He hadn't really lost control of himself except for a moment.

With the opening of the ninth it looked as if Tompkins was right. Troop Five had failed to score further, but Ranny entered the box apparently as cool and self-contained as he had been at the beginning of the game. Quietly and efficiently he took the first batter in hand, and in spite of the joshing that at once began on the other side, he lured the boy into popping up a little infield fly that was easily smothered by the second baseman.

The next fellow up, however, sent out a long fly to right-field which Blair unaccountably muffed. Instantly the shrill, nagging voice of "Red" Conners pierced the din.

"Up in a balloon!" he yelled. "Little Lambie's ready for the stable. He's done. I knew he couldn't stand up before a regular team once we got his number."

Irritating as a mosquito's buzz, the strident voice rasped Dale Tompkins's spirit like a file, and a rush of sympathy for the pitcher swept over him. He knew how annoying it is to be blamed for another's fault, and the error was distinctly Blair's for muffing that fly. If only Phelps wouldn't pay any attention to the nagging! He had only to put out two more men and win the game. Surely he must realize that the fellows didn't mean anything they said; that they were only trying–

He caught his breath with a swift, anxious intake as the ball left Ranny's fingers and an instant later went sailing over the infield. It was a clean hit and brought forth a roar of delight from Troop One's adherents, who at once redoubled their efforts to tease the angry pitcher. It wasn't baseball, in its better sense, nor did it show the real scout spirit, but it was human nature. Seeing the game slipping from them, they took the only way they had been able to discover to turn the tables. Ranny, plainly furious, pitched hastily to the next batter and hit him in the arm. The bases were filled, with only one out.

"They've rattled him, all right," said the regretful voice of Paul Trexler at Tompkins's elbow. "Great Scott! He can't be going to stick it out!"

For a moment it looked that way. Flushed and furious, his snapping eyes sweeping the circle of grinning faces, Ranny stood motionless for a moment or two in the middle of the diamond. He even toed the slab and took a signal from Ted MacIlvaine. Then, of a sudden, his arm dropped to his side, and he stalked across the infield toward the bench. By the time he reached it his face was white, save where the grip of teeth had left little crimson dents in his under lip. His level, almost hostile, glance fixed Dale Tompkins coldly.

"Go in, Tompkins," he said curtly, and tossed him the ball.

Dale caught it instinctively, and, scrambling to his feet, pulled off his sweater mechanically. His chance had come, but somehow he did not want it now. He would infinitely rather have had Ranny keep his head and his control and finish the game he had started off so well. The hurt and shame in that white face smote on him with a sense of physical pain, made him feel in a curious, involved fashion as if he were in some manner responsible for the humiliation of his hero.

A moment later all this vanished from his mind as he crossed the diamond, his heart beating unevenly, every sense concentrated in the task before him. He was greeted by a burst of joshing from Conners and the others, but he scarcely heard it. Quite without self-consciousness as he was, the remarks of the crowd, with most of whom he was on friendly terms, meant nothing to him. It was merely an obvious attempt to rattle him to which he paid no heed, so intent was he on gaging the boy who stood, bat in hand, a little to one side of the plate.

Tompkins had warmed up a little before the game, and now, after throwing a few to MacIlvaine, he found the plate and nodded to the batter to resume his place. All the afternoon he had been sizing up the different batters, noting as well as he could the strength and weakness of each one. He thought he knew the sort of ball Jack Dillon could not hit safely, and promptly he proceeded to send it up.

In that very instant something in the fellow's face told him that he had blundered. His heart leaped with the crack of leather meeting wood; he caught his breath almost with a sob as the ball whizzed past his vainly reaching arm. There was no answering thud behind him. Bob Gibson had missed! Heartsick, he saw the runner shoot down from third and cross the plate. Close at his heels, it seemed, the fellow behind him rounded the sack and started home. Suddenly he doubled back, and Dale realized with a gasp of thankfulness that Gardner had nipped that second run with a fine throw to the plate from center-field.

He was trembling a bit as he caught the ball from MacIlvaine and moved slowly backward, turning it nervously in his hands. There was a sick, sinking sensation in the pit of his stomach. All about him the opposition were yelling joyously as if it were only a question of minutes before the game could be counted theirs.

"Another easy mark!" shrilled Conners. "We've got him going, too. One good single, Irish, and we take the lead. Come over here, Blakie, and coach. I'm up next."

Dale brought his teeth down hard and his jaw squared. He'd show Red Conners who was easy. Stepping into the box, he met the confident grin of Roddy Thorpe. This time there could be no mistake. He knew Roddy's game through and through. His eyes dropped to where MacIlvaine crouched, giving a signal from behind his mitt. He shook his head slightly, and Bob, with some reluctance, changed the signal for another. Dale pitched suddenly, and Thorpe, swinging with all his strength to meet the sort of ball he thought was coming, missed, with ludicrous dismay.

He fouled the second one, and then let two go by. Finally he missed again, fooled by a sudden change of pace and a slow ball when he had expected speed. A cheer went up from his team-mates that still further heartened Tompkins.

"Who's an easy mark now, Red?" taunted Frank Sanson, pounding his glove delightedly. "Here's where you get yours, too."

"I should worry!" retorted Conners, dancing to the plate with every sign of confidence. "That was only a fluke; it won't last."

Dale's eyes narrowed a bit as he surveyed the grinning, freckled face before him. Ordinarily, he and Red were on good enough terms, but at this moment he felt a slow, smoldering anger against the fellow who, he felt, had been the main cause of forcing Ranny out of the box. "Here's where I even up," he muttered.

He took Bob's signal, and promptly, yet without apparent haste, he pitched. The ball left his fingers and whistled over with a slight inswerve. Conners swung his bat fiercely, but encountered nothing but empty air.

"One!" muttered Tompkins, under his breath. "Two more, now–just two more!"

The next was a ball, and Conners let it pass. Then came a slow one delivered with a swing and snap that fooled the batter into striking before it was well within his reach. As he regained his balance he scowled slightly and shook his head. The grin still stretched his lips, but it had turned into a grimace.

Dale's heart began to pound. Over and over again he was saying to himself: "One more! Only one more! I must get him–I've got to!"

Silence had fallen on the field. The batter's team-mates had left off their gibing. It seemed as if every fellow gathered about the edges of the diamond was holding his breath.

Dale's right hand drew back slowly, and for an instant he cuddled the ball under his chin. Then, like a flash, his arm shot forward and a gray shadow whizzed through the air.

The ball was high–too high, many a breathless onlooker thought at first. But suddenly it flashed downward across Conner's shoulders. Too late the batter saw it drop and brought his bat around. There was a swish, a thud–and the umpire's voice was drowned in the shrill yell of relaxing tension that split the throats of the victorious team as they made a rush for Tompkins, standing in the middle of the diamond.

Sanson and Bob Gibson reached him first, but the others were not far behind. Thumping, pounding, poking him in the ribs and executing around him an impromptu war-dance, they swept Dale toward the bench, jabbering excitedly the while. In a happy sort of daze the boy heard the hearty congratulations of Mr. Curtis. Then, when the throng had spread out a little, he suddenly found himself face to face with Ranleigh Phelps.

For a second there was an embarrassed silence; then the blond chap put out his hand.

"You did mighty well, Tompkins," he said, with a touch of constraint in his manner. "I wish–" He paused an instant, and a faint color crept into his face. "I'd just like you to know," he went on rapidly, "that I haven't kept you out of the box all season because–because of–wanting to take all the pitching myself. I–I–didn't think you'd make good. I was wrong, of course. I–I'm sorry it's too late to–prove it to you."

That was all. Without waiting for a reply, he turned away. But Dale's face glowed. Somehow those brief words from Ranleigh meant more to him than the exuberant congratulations of all the others.

CHAPTER XVIII

A QUESTION OF MONEY

With the inter-troop baseball series a thing of the past, Sanson and Trexler promptly turned their attention to swimming. They had already been out to the lake several times, but with baseball practise almost every day, it had not been possible to spend very much time there. Now, however, they both took advantage of every free afternoon, and before a great while Paul emerged from that first hopeless, helpless state when it seemed as if he were never going to be able even to support himself in the water. He was still far from being a good swimmer, but at least he could behold the miraculous ease and skill of the other fellows without a feeling of despondent envy.

Frank Sanson naturally made much quicker progress. Knowing the rudiments, he did not, like Paul, have to start at the very beginning. His strength and endurance, too, were greater than his friend's, and he had practically none of Trexler's nervous timidity to combat. All he needed was practise, and he was not long graduating from the novice class.

The latter was uncommonly large this year. It was the first time the boys had had the freedom of Crystal Lake, and practically every scout who did not know how to swim seemed bent on learning before the summer camp started. Many of the enthusiasts went out there every afternoon, while Saturdays always saw a big crowd, most of whom brought their lunch and made a day of it.

As a matter of course, since swimming could not very well be indulged in all the time, there developed a great variety of scout sports and activities. Often a scoutmaster or two showed up, and by dint of a little suggestion would introduce among the purely entertaining games one designed to test the boys' ability at signaling or first aid, or his knowledge of tracking and trailing and woodcraft generally.

The system was entirely successful. Fellows who lacked the ambition or push to acquire these important details of scouting–and there are always such in every troop–found themselves, to their surprise, absorbing the knowledge through the medium of a game or competition. More often than not they discovered that it wasn't so hard or uninteresting as they supposed, and in many cases real enthusiasm developed. Moreover, members of the different troops came to know and understand each other in a way which would have been impossible without this close and constant companionship. Hitherto they had kept pretty much to themselves, each boy traveling mainly with his own crowd and generally meeting the others as opponents on gridiron or diamond.

Now unexpected friendships developed. Paul Trexler, who had revived much of his interest in bird study, was amazed to find a kindred spirit in Jim Crancher of Troop One. This big, rather rough-and-ready, chap of whom Paul had always stood somewhat in awe, proved to be quite as keen as himself about birds and nature generally, and the two had many a pleasant and profitable tramp through the woods together. There were many other similar cases, and before long it was no uncommon thing to see boys who had hitherto been rivals eating their lunch together and chatting intimately about what they would do at camp.

The latter subject became more and more a topic of interest and discussion. For the first time the various troops were planning to join forces in a common camp, and for months a committee of scoutmasters had been at work on the details. Funds for equipment had been secured by the local council, but the question of a proper location threatened to prove a serious difficulty. Dozens of sites had been investigated and found lacking in some important particular, either in quantity or quality of water, in woods not extensive enough for hiking, and the like. Most of the really attractive lakes in that part of the State were lined with summer cottages and bungalows, while the wilder, mountainous sections were too inaccessible to be wisely considered in a camp of this nature.

The boys were beginning to grow seriously worried when suddenly the rumor swept through town that a novel and totally unexpected solution of the difficulty had presented itself. It was said that the committee had been offered the use of a large tract of land in the southern part of the State bordering on the ocean. Such a situation had never been even remotely considered, and the excitement of the boys, many of whom had never seen the ocean, rose to fever-heat at the enthralling possibility.

At the earliest possible moment Troop Five in a body hurried around to obtain further details from Mr. Curtis, only to discover that he had gone with other members of the committee to look the ground over. He was away for three days, returning the afternoon of the troop meeting, from which, it is perhaps needless to say, not a scout was absent.

"You've heard about it, I see," the scoutmaster remarked as he surveyed the line of eager, bright-eyed boys before him. "Well, I don't know that we can employ our time better to-night than in going over the camp proposition thoroughly and finding out what you fellows think of the situation."

"Is it going to be at–at that place on the ocean, sir?" put in one of the boys.

"Yes; we've practically decided to accept Mr. Thornton's offer. The distance was the only drawback; it's almost a hundred miles from here, but I think we can get around that. Everything else is ideal. The land is a wooded point of six or seven hundred acres. One side faces the ocean, the other a wide, sheltered bay that runs inland several miles, joining finally with a small river. The whole point is rather high ground, with stretches of sand-dunes on the ocean side, and wooded with scrub-oak and stunted pines. Back of that, the land is mostly covered with second-growth timber, and rises gradually to an elevation called Lost Mine Hill–"

"What's that, sir?" interrupted Court Parker, eagerly.

The scoutmaster smiled. "At the time of the Revolution there was said to be a copper-mine located thereabouts, the entrance to which has since been lost track of. At least, that's what one of the old residents told us."

More than one boy's eyes sparkled. There was a fascination in the mere name.

"Whether it's true or not, I have no idea," continued Mr. Curtis. "To return to the camp. This would be located on the bay side of the point, facing the village, which is over a mile distant and practically the only settlement around. The beach shelves gradually here, making an ideal place for swimming, and there are three or four small islands about a quarter of a mile from shore. The fishing in the bay is fine, and there are lots of crabs and eels in the coves and inlets farther up. We should have to do a lot of clearing out, of course, for the undergrowth is pretty thick, but that would be more fun than otherwise."

A long, concerted sigh went up from the listening scouts. Ocean and islands and a lost copper-mine seemed too entrancing a combination to be possible. Several boys began to ask questions at once, but stopped at a gesture from Mr. Curtis.

"One at a time, fellows," he reminded them. "The only practicable way of getting there, Bob, is to hire an auto-truck and motor down to Clam Cove, crossing over in a motor-boat. We haven't enough tents or equipment to accommodate all the fellows at once, so we've decided to divide in two or three relays of say thirty-five boys to a group, each crowd to stay two weeks. The truck could make the trip in seven or eight hours, and by starting early could take one bunch down and bring another back the same day, thus considerably lessening the expense."

"How much do you think that will be, sir?" asked Dale Tompkins, quickly, an anxious wrinkle in his forehead.

"About five dollars a week for board and a dollar extra for transportation."

The troubled expression deepened in Dale's face, and he scarcely heard the various other questions and answers that followed. Six dollars a week–twelve in all! There would be other necessities, too, in the way of clothes fit for camp. He had no shorts, for instance, or decent sneakers. Fifteen dollars would barely cover the outlay; and though he had worked hard for two months at least, he had little more than half of the amount saved. Where was the rest to come from?

When Mr. Curtis, with pencil and paper in hand, started at the head of the line to note down what boys were going, Tompkins roused himself and listened with a touch of envy to the ready answers: "Yes, sir!" "You can count me in every time, sir!" "Can't a fellow stay longer than two weeks?" or, from Larry Wilks, "No, sir; I'm going up to Maine as soon as school is over." Not one of them seemed troubled by the problem which worried him.

"How about you, Dale?" asked the scoutmaster, after jotting down Vedder's prompt acquiescence.

"I–don't know, sir."

"What's the trouble? Want to talk it over at home?" said the scoutmaster, dropping his voice.

"N-o, sir. They'll let me go all right," answered Dale, adding, in a still lower tone, "only I–I'm not sure about the–money."

Mr. Curtis nodded understandingly. "I see. Well, there will be at least two weeks before even the first crowd goes. We'll have to get together and think up ways and means."

He passed on, leaving Dale not very greatly encouraged. It would be like Mr. Curtis to invent some work about his place whereby the scout might earn the required amount, but Dale was determined to stay at home rather than take advantage of the scoutmaster in that way.

"He's done enough for me already," the boy said to himself with a stubborn squaring of the jaws. "If I can't raise the funds some other way, I'll just have to go without camp."

That night he lay long awake, trying to think of some possible method, but his efforts were not very successful. He still had his paper-route, but the money from that went mostly into the family treasury. He might, and probably would, get some odd jobs during the next two weeks, but there was only grass cutting, now, or weeding gardens, and neither of these chores was particularly well paid in Hillsgrove.

On the whole the outlook was distinctly discouraging, and for the next few days Dale had a struggle to maintain his usual cheerfulness. For months he had looked forward to camp as the supreme culmination of a more than usually happy year.

"It doesn't seem as if I could give it up!" he muttered rebelliously at the end of a day which had brought him just twenty cents for a laborious weeding job. "Oh, gee! If I'd only started to save for it sooner, I–" He broke off and bit his lips. Presently a crooked smile struggled defiantly through the gloom. "Oh, thunder!" he exclaimed whimsically. "Quit your grouching, Dale Tompkins. If you're going to let a little matter like earning ten dollars stand between you and a corking good time, you're no kind of a scout at all."

CHAPTER XIX

THE ACCIDENT

It was on Thursday morning that Mr. Curtis sent for Dale, and in spite of his suspicions the boy brightened a little as he entered the scoutmaster's study and noticed the smile on the latter's face.

"Well, Dale," began Mr. Curtis, cheerily, "I've been puzzling my brains over that problem of yours ever since Monday night, and yesterday the answer was fairly thrust on me."

The boy pricked up his ears doubtfully. "What is it, sir?" he asked quickly.

"Bird-houses. You're our prize carpenter, and I know you made a number of them in the spring. Now–"

"Bird-houses!" interrupted the boy, incredulously. "Bird-houses at the end of June! Why, who–I'll bet you're making–"

He broke off abruptly, biting his lips. Mr. Curtis did not seem offended. In fact, he merely chuckled and shrugged his shoulders.

"No, it's not that," he said quickly. "I've nothing at all to do with it. I had an inquiry this morning from some one who–a–probably knows it's a scout specialty for a quotation on a number of rather elaborate houses that are wanted at once. There's the list."

Dazedly Dale took the paper and stared at it. It was a type-written list describing, with some detail, the eight bird-houses desired. Two of them, for martin colonies, called for something large and rather elaborate. All were distinctly of a more expensive class than was usually in demand. Even without figuring, he could see that his time alone, were it possible to finish the work inside of two weeks, would be worth over ten dollars. In spite of his doubts, his eyes brightened as he looked up at the scoutmaster.

"It's a corking order!" he exclaimed. "It would put me all to the good. But I can't understand why anybody would want bird-houses after the birds have all nested for the season. Who are they for, sir?"

"That I can't tell you," returned Mr. Curtis. "Now don't go off at half-cock," he added quickly, as Dale's lips parted impulsively. "I've told you I had nothing to do with it in any way. The inquiry this morning was as much of a surprise to me as it is to you, but just because the person doesn't wish to be known is no reason why you should balk at the offer. There may be any number of reasons. At least there's no touch of charity about it. You'll be giving full value received, won't you? And you certainly build better houses than any other boy in the troop."

For a second Dale hesitated, torn between a last lingering doubt and a natural eagerness to snatch at this wonderful opportunity. "You mean you–advise me to accept?" he asked slowly.

"I do. I see no reason why you shouldn't treat it as a regular business proposition and make out your estimate at once."

Dale hesitated no longer. The whole thing still seemed odd, but after all, as Mr. Curtis had said, he had nothing to do with that. He was still further reassured when he went over the specifications again, seated at a corner of the scoutmaster's writing-table. The very detail with which these had been made out pointed to a distinct and definite want, not to a charity meant to give work to an unknown scout.

For two hours the boy sat making rough plans, measuring, figuring, and calculating with the utmost care. He conscientiously put his estimate as low as he possibly could, and when word came next day to go ahead he plunged into the work blithely, determined to give the unknown good value for his money.

Fortunately, school was over and Dale could give practically all his time to the undertaking. He took a chance and registered for the first two weeks at camp, but it was a close call, and the houses were delivered to Mr. Curtis only the very morning before the party was scheduled to start. That afternoon he had the money, and there was no happier boy in Hillsgrove as he hastily sought the scout store at the Y. M. C. A. and made his necessary purchases.

It was at the same place that the crowd gathered with bag and baggage next morning at six o'clock. Early as it was, the majority were on hand before the appointed hour, so there was no delay in getting off. Seats had been built along each side of the big motor-truck, and the moment suitcases and duffle-bags were stowed away beneath them, there was a scramble to get aboard.

Tompkins found himself presently squeezed in near the rear, next to Court Parker, with Sanson, Bob Gibson, and Paul Trexler near by. Most of the older fellows were farther front, and Mr. Curtis sat next to the driver. It was a perfect day, clear, sparkling, cloudless, and as the truck rumbled out of Hillsgrove and started southward along the fine state road the boys were in high spirits. Soon some one started up a song, and from one familiar air they passed to another, letting off a good deal of steam in that fashion. A lot more was got rid of by practising troop yells, and when the truck began to pass between fields of waving yellow grain, they found amusement in seeing how many of the laboring farmers would answer their shouts and hand-wavings.

But it wasn't possible, of course, to keep up this sort of thing for the entire journey, and after a couple of hours they settled down to a quieter key. Naturally, the most interesting subject of discussion was the camp, and presently, in response to a number of requests, Mr. Curtis moved back to the middle of the truck to tell the crowd, that included many boys from other troops, all he knew about it. When he had described in detail the situation and its advantages and explained the arrangement of the camp which three other scoutmasters and a number of the other boys had gone down ahead to lay out, he paused for a moment or two.

"There's just one thing, fellows," he went on presently "that we've got to be mighty careful about. The land is owned by John Thornton, the banker, whose wonderful country-place, twenty miles this side of Clam Cove, you may have heard about. It seems that he's had a great deal of trouble with boys trespassing, starting fires in the woods, injuring the shrubbery and rare trees, and even trapping game. It's possible, of course, though I should hate to believe it, that some of this damage has been done by scouts, as he seems to think. At all events, he is very much opposed to the movement, which he contends merely gives boys a certain freedom and authority to roam the woods,–building fires, cutting trees, and having a thoughtless good time generally,–without teaching them anything of real value."

"Humph!" sniffed Sherman Ward, indignantly. "Then why has he offered us this camping-site?"

"He hasn't offered it to us as scouts. He's loaned it to Captain Chalmers, who is a very close friend, and he as much as says that our behavior there will merely prove his point about the uselessness of scouting. Of course, he's dead wrong, but he's a mighty hard man to convince, and we'll have to toe the mark all the time. I don't mean it's going to interfere with our having all the fun that's going, but we'll have to take a little more pains than usual to have a model camp. There mustn't be any careless throwing about of rubbish. In getting fire-wood we'll have to put into practice all we've learned about the right sort of forestry. When away from camp on hikes or for any other purpose, we must always conduct ourselves as good scouts and remember that it's not only our own reputation we're upholding, but that of the whole order."

When he had gone back to his place in front there were a few indignant comments on Mr. Thornton and his point of view, but for the most part the boys took it sensibly, with many a determined tightening of the lips.

"I guess he won't get anything on us," commented Ted MacIlvaine, decidedly. "It'll be rather fun, fellows, making him back down."

There was an emphatic chorus of agreement, but little further discussion, for the question of lunch was beginning to be pressing. Though barely eleven, boxes and haversacks were produced and the next half-hour enlivened with one of the most satisfying of occupations. Toward noon they stopped at a small town for "gas." When the car started on again, there was a pleasant sense of excitement in the realization that another couple of hours ought to bring them to Clam Cove.

The country had changed greatly from that around Hillsgrove. It looked wilder, more unsettled. Instead of fields of ripening grain, orchards, or acres of truck-gardens, the road was bordered by long stretches of woods and tangled undergrowth. The farm-houses were farther apart and less pretentious. There was even a faint tang of salt in the air. At length, from the summit of an elevation, Mr. Curtis pointed out a distant hill showing hazily blue on the horizon.

The car crashed into the weather-worn railing of the bridge

"That's Lost Mine Hill, fellows!" he said. "From there, it's not more than three miles to our stopping-place."

Eagerly they stared and speculated as the truck clattered down the incline, its horn sounding raucously. At the bottom there was a straight level stretch of a thousand feet or so, with a bridge midway along it. It was sandy here in the hollow, and the truck had made little more than half the distance to the bridge when all at once, with a weird wailing of the siren, a great gray car shot into sight around a curve beyond.

It was going very fast. Dale and Court, hanging over the side of the truck together, had barely time to note the trim chauffeur behind the wheel and a man and woman in the luxurious tonneau when the explosion of a blow-out, sharp as a pistol-shot, smote on their startled senses. The car leaped, quivered, skidded in the loose sand, crashed into the weather-worn railing of the bridge, hung suspended for an instant above the stream, and then toppled over and out of sight. There was a tremendous splash, a great spurt of flying water, and then–silence!

CHAPTER XX

FIRST AID

Dale never knew just how he got out of the truck. Gripped by the horror and suddenness of the accident, his mind was a blank until he found himself running over the bridge amid a throng of other hurrying scouts. A moment later he was pressed close to the unbroken portion of the railing, and, staring down, caught a glimpse of the gray car upturned in the sluggish waters of the stream.

The car had turned turtle, and the great wheels, still spinning slowly, showed above the surface almost to their hubs. The water was roiled and muddy; bubbles and a little steam rose about the forward part of the car. Ten feet away floated a chauffeur's cap. Nearer at hand, a light lap-robe, billowed by the air caught underneath, seemed for an instant to be the clothing of one of the passengers. But Dale swiftly understood its real nature, and with a choke he realized that the people were pinned beneath the car. All this came to him in a flash; then, as Mr. Curtis and the foremost of the scouts plunged down into the wide, but shallow, stream, he turned suddenly about and raced back to the truck.

It wasn't the sick sense of horror that moved him. All at once he had remembered the troop first-aid kit, which he himself had carefully stowed away under one of the long seats. They would need it badly, and he did not think any of the others had stopped to get it. There would be plenty of them without him to lift the car.

Panting to the side of the deserted truck, Dale leaped into the back, and, dropping to his knees, tore and dug among the close-packed baggage like a terrier seeking rats. Swiftly he unearthed the square, japanned case and dragged it forth. When he reached the bridge again, the scene had altogether changed. Waist-deep in the water, a line of scouts was holding up the heavy car, whose weight was testified to by their straining muscles and tense attitudes. Already the two passengers had been dragged forth. The one whom at first they had taken to be a woman had been carried to the bank, and Dale saw, with a throb of pity, that she was a girl of not more than fifteen. Two scouts supported the limp figure of the man, and as Dale ran around the end of the bridge and down the bank a shout from Sherman Ward announced the discovery of the chauffeur.

"Get him out quickly!" tersely ordered Mr. Curtis. "You and Crancher look after him; you know what to do. Bob and Ranny see to the girl! I'll take care of this man. Court, hustle for the first-aid kit; it's under– Oh, you've got it! Good boy, Dale. Open it upon the bank and get out the ammonia. Then be ready with some bandages when I call for them. Frank, take one or two fellows and bring six or eight blankets here from the truck."

Under the cool, dominating influence of the scoutmaster the situation speedily resolved itself into one of orderly method. The three patients were stretched out on blankets on the bank, and only those scouts actively interested in bringing them around were allowed in the vicinity. The others went back to the car and busied themselves with trying to right it–a rather futile undertaking, but it kept them out of the way.

The girl was the first to respond to treatment, but the older man opened his eyes not long afterward. While both were dazed by the shock, they seemed to have escaped with no more serious injuries than bruises. The chauffeur, however, was badly cut about the face and head, and Mr. Curtis himself superintended the work of Ward and Crancher in tying up and bandaging. When this was over he turned back to the other man, who was trying to get on his feet.

"Hadn't you better lie quietly for a bit longer?" he asked quickly. "You've been rather badly shaken up."

"Is Robert–all right?" asked the other, briefly, as he dropped back to the ground again.

"Practically. He's cut about the head, but we've bandaged him up, and I think he'll be all right until we can get him to a doctor."

The man's puzzled gaze wandered to the little group of scouts standing well to one side and then returned to Mr. Curtis's face. "I don't understand how you came to be on the spot so promptly," he murmured. "Who–"

"My name is Curtis," explained the scoutmaster, as the other paused. "I'm taking a party of scouts from Hillsgrove down to camp on Great Bay. Our truck wasn't a hundred feet away when you skidded."

The older man raised his eyebrows.

"Scouts!" he repeated. "Boy Scouts?" Again his glance swept the circle, taking in this time the prone figure of the chauffeur, whose head, swathed in workmanlike bandages, rested against a thin roll of blanket. "I understand," he went on briefly. "I am very greatly indebted to you, Mr. Curtis. May I trouble you?"

He extended his hand, and this time the scoutmaster did not hesitate to help him up. Together the two assisted the girl to her feet, and Mr. Curtis reached for a blanket, placing it carefully around her shoulders.

"Thank you," she murmured shyly. She had recovered from her fright, and seemed none the worse for the accident. "Dad, if we could only get a car or something to take us home," she said pluckily.

"Our truck isn't exactly comfortable," suggested Mr. Curtis, "but I fancy it would be the quickest way."

"Decidedly!" agreed the man. "The nearest house is two miles off, and my own place isn't more than double that. But wouldn't it be inconveniencing you?"

"Not a bit! We have plenty of time; and anyway, your man ought to have a doctor's attention as soon as possible. The boys can wait here till the truck comes back."

Without further delay he motioned Ward and Crancher to help the chauffeur and led the way to the truck. Full of interest and curiosity, the others watched them take their places, saw the engine started, and remained staring after the lumbering vehicle until it had passed out of sight around the curve. Then began an eager discussion of the whole affair, until finally some one suggested building a fire and drying out their wet clothes. The latter process was still going on when the truck returned, after nearly an hour's absence, and Mr. Curtis leaped out. As he came up to the group he was smiling.

"Who was it, sir?" called several of the scouts at once. "Did you find out?"

"I did." The scoutmaster's smile deepened a little. "You can have three guesses."

There was a moment's puzzled silence; then, "Mr. Thornton?" hazarded Court Parker, flippantly.

"Not quite," laughed Mr. Curtis; "only his brother and niece."

Parker gasped in surprise; so did several others. Then a shout went up, and a volley of questions was poured at the scoutmaster.

"Did you meet Mr. Thornton?"

"Does he still think scouting isn't any good?"

"He failed to say," returned Mr. Curtis, his eyes twinkling. "I hoped, of course, that he'd fall on my neck and declare he was all wrong and that scouting was the most wonderful thing in the world. But apparently he isn't that sort. There's no question, though, that he was favorably impressed, and with this good beginning I trust we can bring him around before camp is over. Pile in now, fellows. We're late already and mustn't waste any more time."

About an hour afterward they rumbled over a bridge, ran along a rather sluggish stream for a quarter of a mile or so, and then entered the little village of Clam Cove, where they found Captain Chalmers and Mr. Knox, one of the scoutmasters, somewhat impatiently awaiting them. Full of excitement, the boys piled out, gathered up their luggage, and made tracks for the two motor-boats tied to the end of the dock. There was the usual bustle and turmoil of embarking, but no delay, for every one was too anxious to see the camp to waste any time stowing himself away. In ten minutes the entire crowd was disposed of and the ropes cast off.

The bay was over a mile wide at this point. Its waters, stirred into ripples by the freshening breeze, glinted in the rays of the afternoon sun. Against the dark green of the farther shore a string of little islands showed and started a buzz of eager comment and question. About half-way across, the camp itself came suddenly into sight, a trim row of glistening white tents outlined against a background of fir and cedar, which brought forth a shout of delight.

"Gee! Don't it look great? I can hardly believe we're here, can you?"

But there could be no question of the reality of it all as they tumbled into the trailers and went ashore in relays. It was a rather small point, jutting out from the larger one into the comparatively quiet waters of the bay. For some distance back the undergrowth had been cleared away, but clumps of bushy cedars and glossy-leaved holly remained to give shade and diversity. Six wall-tents, each with a wooden floor and bunks to accommodate eight boys, were pitched on two sides of a square, at the corner of which stood a larger tent known as headquarters. Here dwelt the governing powers, in the shape of the commissioner and the three scoutmasters, and in front of it, on a rustic pole fluttered the Stars and Stripes. Across the square, among the trees, was a large dining-tent, and behind that a substantial frame cook-shack.

To the new arrivals, hot and dusty from their long ride, it all looked tremendously cool and inviting, and there was a rush to shed uniforms and get into shorts and undershirts. Dale Tompkins found himself placed in a tent with Court Parker, Sanson, Bob Gibson, Trexler, Vedder and Bennie Rhead, with Ranleigh Phelps as leader. The latter's presence rather surprised him. He supposed Ranny would want to be with Torrance and Slater, two of his closest chums. Later, learning that Wesley Becker was tent-leader with that crowd, he decided that the arrangement was due to the camp heads rather than to Ranny's personal preference.

But no matter what the cause, Tompkins was distinctly glad of the other's presence. Though he tried not to build any hopes on what might be merely the result of his own imagination, Dale had a feeling that the fellow he admired and liked in spite of himself hadn't been quite so distant lately. Besides, offish or not, just having Ranny in the same tent seemed, curiously, to bring him nearer, and Dale settled himself in the opposite bunk with an odd thrill of satisfaction.

Long before the hour for the afternoon swim the fellows were in their bathing togs, impatiently awaiting the signal. When it came, there was a regular stampede down to the beach, and in the space of thirty seconds every scout, save only three of the advance-party, who had been appointed life-savers, was splashing joyously in the water. They enjoyed every minute of that half-hour, and responded to the dressing signal with a reluctance that was considerably tempered by Mr. Reed's announcement of an early supper.

There was no council-fire that night. The crowd that had come down was too sleepy to do more than listen to a brief talk by Captain Chalmers in front of headquarters tent, in which he repeated what Mr. Curtis had told them of the need of refuting Mr. Thornton's peculiar ideas on scouting and briefly explained the camp rules and routine.

Each of the six tents, which were numbered, was to be daily assigned to special duty such as sanitary squad, cook's helpers, commissary, and the like. In addition there would be a daily tent-inspection, and before each meal an inspection of the tables, which corresponded to the tents in number and for which the boys occupying those tents were responsible. All of these marks would be carefully kept, and the tent having the highest at the end of each week would be the honor tent, to be accorded special privileges besides having its individual marks go toward the winning of a camp emblem. This emblem, the captain explained, would be the highest honor a scout could obtain in camp, and when he had finished, almost every one of his hearers was keenly determined to carry the coveted trophy back to Hillsgrove on the front of his jersey.

It was barely dark when the talk was over, but already more than one tired scout was nodding and the clear notes of taps sent them stumbling tentward. Dale Tompkins lost not a moment in shedding his clothes and crawling in between the blankets. He heard vaguely the complaining tones of Harry Vedder as he climbed into an upper bunk, and the joshing comment of those who watched the diverting process. But even these sounds barely penetrated to his brain. In a moment more he was lost to the world, and in his next conscious moment he was opening his eyes to the dawn of another day.

CHAPTER XXI

LOST MINE HILL

The camp was very still. Each tree and bush stood motionless and distinct in the queer gray light of early morning. Their tent was the last in the row, and lying on his side, Dale could look under the rolled-up flap straight across the sloping, sandy beach, over the smooth, rhythmic lapping water of the bay to the low, sparsely wooded line beyond which lay the sea. There was a crisp tang to the air that made him snuggle into his blankets as he drowsily watched the eastern sky turn pink and gold and delicately crimson in the glory of the rising sun.

The boy gave a sigh of content, and his lids drooped sleepily. The next thing he knew reveille was sounding, and he rolled over to meet the glance of Ranny Phelps, sitting tousle-headed on the edge of the opposite bunk.

"Gee! Isn't this great!" exclaimed Tompkins, impulsively.

Ranny nodded. "It sure is!" he agreed, in a half-friendly, half-embarrassed fashion. And then, almost as if regretting his tone, he sprang up and reached for his swimming-tights. "Everybody out for the morning dip, fellows," he called authoritatively.

They needed no urging. Vedder was the only one who clung to his blankets, and the others lost no time in dragging these off and applying the sole of a sneaker with a dexterity that brought a howl of protest from the plump youth.

"Ouch! Quit that!" he roared, rolling over the side of the bunk and thudding to the floor. "Wait till I get hold of you, Court Parker, and I'll–"

The threat ended in a sputter as the rest fled, giggling, to gather before headquarters for the brief ceremony of flag-raising. Then followed five minutes of setting-up exercises that sent the blood tingling through their veins and made them more than ever eager for the refreshing plunge, after which came dressing, the airing of blankets, and breakfast–and the day's work and pleasure had fairly begun.

It was mostly work that first morning. Dale's tent had pioneering duties, and for two hours or more he sweated with ax and grub-hoe, clearing out more undergrowth and making the camp shipshape. Ranny was no easy taskmaster. He kept everybody hustling without any let-up, and half an hour before inspection he had the whole seven hard at work on the tent, sweeping, folding blankets, and tidying up generally. There were a few grumbling asides, but the credit they received at the inspection silenced all that and made each boy resolved to be just as thorough every day. It wasn't so bad, after all, most of them decided. Certainly they enjoyed their swim twice as much for the knowledge that the longest part of the day lay before them, unburdened by a single duty.

Both before and during dinner, there was a good deal of speculation as to what had been planned for the afternoon. But this was not revealed until the last spoonful of dessert had been consumed, when Mr. Reed arose from his place at the officers' table.

"Most of you fellows have heard of Lost Mine Hill," he said, "and are probably wanting to get a closer view of it. There's a legend, you know, that before the Revolution there were copper workings in the neighborhood which were long ago abandoned and the entrance to the shafts, or whatever they were, lost track of. This afternoon we'll take a hike over there and see if a little systematic scouting can't solve the mystery. To make it more interesting, we'll consider it a sort of competition on the treasure-hunt idea, each tent working together as a unit against the other five. If the entrance should happen to be located, the crowd that finds it will be given a certain number of credits toward the emblem. Everybody be on hand at headquarters at one sharp, for we don't want to waste any time starting."

The idea met with instant approval, and the burst of eager talk that followed showed how thoroughly it had stirred the boys' imaginations. For the next twenty minutes the camp buzzed with interested discussion, and at one o'clock not a scout was missing from the throng before headquarters tent.

They started at once, with Mr. Reed and Mr. Curtis in the lead. There were no regular roads to follow, but after half an hour's tramp through the woods they struck an overgrown track, and kept to it until it simply dwindled away into nothing and disappeared. A little distance beyond, the ground began to rise, gradually at first, but with increasing steepness, while outcroppings of rock showed more and more frequently. Presently, reaching a small open place among the trees, the scoutmasters paused and waited for the stragglers to come up.

"We may as well start the hunt here, fellows," said Mr. Reed, taking out his watch. "I won't make any suggestions as to how to go about it; each tent-leader must think that out for himself. Use your heads, that's all, and don't get too far away to be back here at four-thirty sharp. It's taken us over an hour to make this point, so we ought to start back then at the latest. Remember, a little blazing will make the return trip easier, and if nobody finds anything to-day, we'll take it up later in the week. Go ahead."

The boys had been standing in little groups about him, and at the signal most of these started off hotfoot, as if they expected to gain their end by speed alone. Some hurried on toward the summit of the hill; others turned to right or left and, pushing through the undergrowth, disappeared along the side of the slope. Somewhat to Tompkins's surprise, Ranny Phelps dawdled along until the others were out of sight. Then, however, he turned swiftly and led the way almost directly downhill.

"What are you going back for?" asked Court Parker, in surprise.

"I've got a hunch," returned Ranny, briefly. Though instantly besieged with questions, he did not continue until they were well away from the clearing.

"It's just this," he said, without moderating his brisk pace. "We certainly can't expect to find something that even the natives have lost track of, by just tramping around aimlessly. Of course, we might happen to stumble on it, but that would be a thousand-to-one chance. The best way is to use system. Did any of you notice the old fellow who brought over a load of fish this morning?"

"The man with whiskers you were talking to at the cook-shack?" asked Frank Sanson.

"Yes. Well, he's lived around here all his life and is quite a character. I was asking him about this lost mine just out of curiosity and without having heard anything about the stunt this afternoon. He didn't know much, but he finally did say his grandfather had once told him of an old building they used as a smelter, or something."

"Gee!" exclaimed Sanson, excitedly. "And is this the way to it?"

"He hadn't any idea. He'd never seen it himself, and of course it must have gone to ruin ages ago. But it stands to reason, doesn't it, that a smelter would be more on the level and not on the side of a hill like this? They'd have to cart stuff to and from it along some kind of a road–"

"The one we came along!" put in Parker, eagerly.

"Maybe, though no road would keep open all this time without cutting. Very likely that's just a lumbering-track. The point is, if we can only locate this building, we'll be somewhere near the mine and won't have to go prospecting all over the map. So that's what we want to look for–a foundation of any kind or the least sign of a building. As soon as we're down a bit farther we'll spread out and hunt systematically. It may be clear on the other side of the hill, but at least we'll have something definite to look for."

"I'll bet it's on this side," said Dale Tompkins, suddenly. "In the old days they didn't have many roads and did most of their traveling by water, so I should think– Oh, shucks! I forgot the smelter would be near the mine and that might be anywhere."

"It might," agreed Ranny; "but it won't do any harm to try this side first."

Full of enthusiasm, they hurried down the slope, and when the steepest part was over they spread out in a line about twenty feet apart. In this formation they moved forward, keeping a sharp lookout for the slightest sign that might help them in the search.

They moved slowly forward through the forest, the fascination of the hunt gripping them more and more strongly. The sense of emulation, always keen with a crowd of boys, was intensified by the belief that, thanks to Ranny, they had just a little better chance of success than any of the others. The object of their search, too, stirred the imagination. There was a glamour of mystery about it which placed the whole thing in a different class from the games that they ordinarily played.

But little by little, as they found only the same monotonous succession of rocks and trees and tangled undergrowth, Dale's mind began to dwell on the growing probability that they might not find the mine after all. Over an hour of close search had failed to reveal any trace of the ruined smelter. The ground on the river side of the hill had been thoroughly gone over, and they were now making their way inland, keeping well in toward the slope, and even spreading out a little on it. Without actually running into any of the other searching-parties, they had twice heard voices farther up the hill. The second time, in fact, these were so near that Dale could distinguish the familiar tones of Wesley Becker, and it was while peering curiously through the trees in that direction that he tripped over an obstruction and fell headlong, bruising his shin and twisting one wrist painfully.

"You want to look out for those feet of yours, Tommy," laughed Frank Sanson, from the right. "They're awful things to trip over."

Usually quick enough with a retort, Tompkins made no answer. He had scrambled up and stood clutching his aching wrist instinctively. But neither his gaze nor his attention was on the injured member. Flushed, bright-eyed, he was staring eagerly at the obstacle that had caused his tumble.

It was nothing more than a line of stones, barely showing above the decaying vegetation of the forest floor. But the boy's swift vision had already taken in the fact that the line was straight and true, and that the stones were held together by crumbling remains of mortar.

CHAPTER XXII

AROUND THE COUNCIL FIRE

Dale's first impulse was to summon the others with a jubilant shout. His lips parted swiftly, but closed again as he remembered the nearness of Wes Becker's crowd. It would never do to let them suspect.

"Frank!" he called in a low tone. "Come over here–quick!"

Sanson responded instantly "Found anything?" he demanded, as he plunged through the bushes. Then his eyes fell on the line of ruined masonry and he caught his breath. "Gee!" he exclaimed delightedly. "That certainly looks like–"

"Sh-h!" cautioned Tompkins. "Wes and his bunch are not far off–right up the hill: we mustn't put them wise, or they'll all come piling down here. You get Ranny and Court, and I'll tell the others."

They quickly separated, and in less than three minutes the others had hastened to the spot. As he took in the bit of old wall Ranny Phelps' eyes brightened and he looked at Tompkins.

"I guess you've hit it, old man," he said warmly. "There'd hardly be any other foundation in this jungle. Let's scrape away the leaves and mold a little and see if we can't find a corner."

Eagerly they fell to work, and before long had uncovered two sides of a rough stone rectangle, some eighteen by thirty feet, and even unearthed the ends of a couple of tough, hand-hewn oak beams which had fallen in and become covered with dead leaves and other debris. About the middle of one side was a solid, square mass of stone that looked as if it might have been the base of a forge or smelting-furnace. But there was no chance to proceed further, for Ranny suddenly jerked out his watch and gave an exclamation of dismay.

"Gosh! Almost four o'clock. We've got to start back right away."

"Aw–gee! Let's take just a few minutes more," begged several voices at once.

"Nothing doing," returned Ranny, decidedly. "If we're not back at four-thirty, they'll think we've found something, and we don't want that. We've got something definite to start from next time; and if we keep it to ourselves, we'll have a fine and dandy chance of putting it over on the rest of the camp. Everybody get busy and hustle some leaves and stuff over the wall so nobody else'll stumble on it by accident."

In a very short time practically all traces of their explorations had been covered over, and the fellows started back at a brisk pace. They were able to return much more quickly than they had come out, and reached the meeting-place in good season to find, with not a little secret satisfaction, that none of the other parties had met with success.

"But you fellows mustn't let that discourage you," said Mr. Reed, briskly. "As I told you before, you can't expect to locate in an hour or so something that's been lost for nearly a hundred years. We'll try it again about Saturday, and–"

"Aw, Mr. Reed," piped up Bennie, eagerly, "can't we come back to-morrow and–"

He broke off with some abruptness as Ranny's fingers closed over his shoulder in a warning grip. The scoutmaster laughed and shook his head.

"You've got it bad, Bennie," he smiled. "Were you getting warm just when you had to stop? You'll have to practise patience, I'm afraid. To-morrow we're going up the river for crabs, and on Friday afternoon there'll be an athletic meet. Don't worry, though. The mine isn't going to run away."

"You chump!" whispered Phelps in the small boy's ear as they started off downhill in a body. "Do you want to give the whole show away?"

"I didn't mean anything, Ranny–honest. I didn't think–"

"I should say you didn't!" Ranny's tone was severe, but his face relaxed a bit at the other's comical expression of dismay. "Don't let another peep like that out of you or we'll have some of the crowd trailing us next time we come here. I'll be surprised if Wes or somebody hasn't caught on already."

But apparently no one had. Doubtless they laid Bennie's outburst to the irresponsibility of extreme youth and ignored it. On the way back to camp there was a good deal of general discussion and theorizing about the location of the mine, but the members of Tent Three managed their answers well enough, apparently, to prevent suspicion. After supper, too, the interest shifted to the morrow's doings, and by the time the call for council-fire sounded through the dusk Lost Mine had been momentarily forgotten.

Out on the extreme tip of Long Point a great heap of branches and driftwood had been assembled, and around this the scouts gathered in a wide circle. Some sat cross-legged, draped in blankets, for the air was brisk and cool. Others sprawled at length upon the soft sand, shoulder pressing shoulder, arms flung carelessly about one another's neck. Overhead the sky was brilliant with stars. From all about came the soft lapping of water, mingled with the lulling, rhythmic beat of surf upon the distant shore. It was a moment of complete relaxation after a long and strenuous day, and from many lips there breathed sighs of utter contentment.

And then the flames, creeping from a little pile of timber at the bottom of the heap, licked up through the dead branches to flare out at the top–a great yellow beacon that chased away the shadows and brought into clear relief the circle of eager, boyish faces. From where the officers sat came presently the soft chords of Captain Chalmers's guitar mingled with the sweeter, higher tinkle of Mr. Reed's mandolin, feeling their way from simple harmonies into the stirring melody of an old, familiar song. Of course the fellows caught it up, singing lustily to the last note, and their clear young voices, wafting out across the water, reached the ears of a grizzled fisherman coming in with the tide and carried him in a twinkling back fifty years or more into the long-forgotten past.

CHAPTER XXIII

A SURPRISE FOR VEDDER

It was a distinctly informal council-fire. There were no special stunts or games or competitions, as there would be later; merely songs, a few announcements, and finally, as the fire died down to glowing embers, a story or two. But Dale Tompkins had rarely been more perfectly content.

Drawn together, perhaps, by the events of the afternoon and by the interesting secret they held in common, the members of Tent Three were gathered in a group on one side of the circle. Whether by accident or design, Dale sat close to Ranny and a little behind him, where he could watch the play of light and shadow on the leader's handsome face. Scarcely a word passed between them, but Dale was conscious of something in the other's manner which made him wonder, with a thrill, whether the hateful barrier that had existed for so long between them wasn't growing a shade less formidable. Suppose some day it should vanish altogether! Suppose the time came when they could be real friends of the sort he had always dreamed about! He told himself that it was probably all imagination, but this did not take away his pleasure in the picture. And when Ranny, lazily shifting his lounging attitude, leaned carelessly back against the knees of the boy behind him, Dale thrilled to the touch almost as much as he would have done had he not felt the other to be quite unconscious of his presence.

The routine of the second morning in camp was much the same as the first had been. But directly after dinner the fellows piled into boats and rowed out to where the Aquita was anchored. As many as the power-boat would hold went aboard, leaving the rest, with a large assortment of crab-nets, hooks, lines, bait-boxes, and the like, in the trailers. They made a hilarious bunch as they chugged upstream past the straggling fishing-village, under the bridge, and on between the low banks of sedge and tough water-growth that lined the little river. But the noise was as nothing compared with the racket that began when they anchored and dispersed for the afternoon sport.

Some took to the boats, others went ashore and fished from the bank, while a few stayed on the Aquita. The tide was out and it was an ideal spot for crabbing. In fact, the creatures were so plentiful that many of the boys abandoned the slower, more cautious method of luring them to the surface with bait, and took to scooping them off the bottom with nets, to the accompaniment of excited shouts and yells and much splashing of mud and water. They kept at it for about two hours, and when the whistle summoned them back to the motor-boat they brought along a catch big enough to furnish several meals for the entire camp.

The last boat to come in was rowed by Dale Tompkins. Sanson and Bennie Rhead were with him, besides one or two others; but the interest and attention of those gathered on and about the Aquita was swiftly centered on Harry Vedder, perched precariously on the stern seat. His fat legs were drawn up clumsily under him, his pudgy hands tightly gripped the sides of the craft, while his plump face was set in lines expressive of anything but joy.

"What's the matter, Puffy?" called Ranny Phelps, as they approached. "You look like Humpty Dumpty sitting on a wall!"

Vedder merely sniffed poutingly. The faces of Tompkins and Sanson expanded in wide grins. "It's the crabs," chuckled the latter. "They're so fond of him they won't let him alone. You see," he added, his eyes dancing, "some of 'em happened to get out of the box, and the minute they saw Humpty they got terribly attached to him."

"Yes!" snorted the plump youth indignantly–"to one of my legs, the beastly things! Hurry up, Dale, for goodness' sake; I'm all cramped up!"

A snicker went up from the other boats. "You ought to have spoken to 'em sharply, Ved," grinned Ranny, "and discouraged such liberties."

"Yes," laughed Court; "be firm with 'em!"

Vedder snorted again and, reaching for the rail of the Aquita, climbed aboard with remarkable agility. "Maybe you think that's funny," he growled, taking possession of the most comfortable seat in sight; "but I'd rather tackle a snake any day than a boat-load of crabs."

He was so taken up with his own affairs that he quite missed the meaning glance that passed between Court Parker and Bob Gibson as they fastened their painter to the stern of the power-boat. He thought nothing, either, of the fact that they were first ashore, where, hastening to remove from under one of the seats a medium-sized bait-box covered with seaweed, they disappeared behind the cook-shack.

But later on, an uncomfortable suspicion came to him that there was something in the wind. Approaching the cook-shack, where a crowd was occupied in breaking up shells and extracting crab-meat for supper, he noticed Parker, Sanson, and Tompkins giggling and whispering with heads close together. As he came up they stopped abruptly, but after supper he saw them again, clustered in a group with Gibson and Bennie Rhead, and caught a grinning glance from the latter that deepened his suspicion.

"I'll bet they're up to some trick," he said to himself.

Uneasily, he kept a sharp lookout, determined that they should not catch him napping. But oddly enough, the joke, whatever it was, seemed to subside, and for all his watchfulness Vedder failed to detect any more suspicious confabs during the evening.

Nevertheless, he remained on guard, especially after dark. He did not stray far from headquarters without peering about for such pitfalls as taut ropes, water-pails, and the like. At the council-fire he selected his place with especial care, and saw that no one approached from behind without his knowing it. But the evening passed uneventfully, and when he had reached the tent in safety and was undressing by the light of the single lantern, he decided he must have been worrying to no purpose.

"Guess I was wrong after all," he thought, tying the pajama-strings about his ample waist. "My, but bed's going to feel good!"

If there was one thing Vedder took pains about, it was in the arrangement of his blankets. To avoid the unpleasant exposure of toes he had worked out an elaborate system of folds and safety-pins until the combination resembled a sleeping-bag more than anything else. It was his habit to attend to this immediately after supper so that at bedtime there need be no shivery delay in getting fixed for the night. This evening he climbed ponderously to his perch, inwardly congratulating himself on his forethought, for the others, chattering busily on the day's doings, were only beginning to spread out their blankets.

"It pays to be systematic," he thought complacently, and thrust his legs between the warm folds with a luxurious sigh of content.

An instant later a howl of terror resounded through the camp, followed by a convulsive movement of Vedder's legs and body which disrupted the neat arrangement in a flash. Dale Tompkins, sitting on the edge of the lower bunk, had no time even to roll aside before the fat boy, still gurgling with fright, landed on him with a crash that shook the tent.

CHAPTER XXIV

THE MISSING SCOUT

"What the mischief is the matter with you?" demanded Tompkins, rubbing his head where it had come into violent contact with the floor.

"A snake!" palpitated Vedder, from the entrance of the tent, to which he had fled. "There's a snake in my bed!"

"You're crazy with the heat, Puffy!" exclaimed Ranny Phelps, forcibly. "How could a snake get into your bunk?"

"It's there, just the same," panted Vedder, his eyes bulging. "When I put my feet down they hit against something cold and–and slimy that squirmed about. Ugh! If I hadn't got out so quick, it would have bit me sure as anything. You look and see, if you don't believe me."

By this time the camp was astir. As Ranny took the lantern and went over to Vedder's bunk, several boys from neighboring tents crowded in to see what was up. When they learned the nature of the rumpus they were vastly more excited than the other occupants of Tent Three, who seemed strangely unaffected by the situation.

"Hanged if there isn't something here!" said Ranny, in a puzzled tone, looking down on the blankets. "Get a couple of sticks, fellows, and some of you hold down the edges of the blankets so it can't get out."

Court Parker turned his back suddenly and choked oddly; Tompkins's face was flushed and twitching. But the new-comers obeyed the order with enthusiasm, and two of them, darting out, returned in a few moments with a couple of crab-nets and the heavy butt of a fishing-rod. Meanwhile, Ranny and several others had drawn the blankets taut across the bunk, revealing an irregular bulge down near the foot that certainly moved slightly.

"Everybody hit together when I give the word," said Ranny. "One, two–three!"

The sticks descended with vigor, and there was a violent wriggling and thrashing about beneath the blankets. But the blows came thick and fast, and in a moment or two all movement ceased.

"I guess it's dead, whatever it is," said Ranny, just as Mr. Reed and Mr. Curtis appeared behind Vedder, still standing prudently in the background. "Let's open it up and have a look."

As he turned down the blankets, the boys gripped their sticks tighter, ready for instant action in case the reptile were not quite dead. But when a final twitch exposed the cause of the commotion, there was a moment's silence, followed by a united exclamation of surprise and disappointment.

"Why, it's nothing but an eel!"

Instantly a yell of laughter went up. Parker and several other occupants of the tent rolled on their bunks in paroxysms of delight. The two scoutmasters, smiling broadly, slipped away. Vedder, jaws agape, stared at Ranny as if unable to believe his hearing.

"An–eel?" he gasped.

"That's all," grinned Ranny. "You've got the whole camp stirred up over a blooming eel instead of a snake."

The fat boy's teeth came together with a click, and, with face flaming, he flounced over to his bunk. "You fellows put it there!" he accused angrily.

"Oh, never!" chuckled Frank Sanson. "I'll bet it got fond of you, like the crabs, and climbed up there to make friends. And now they've gone and smashed the poor thing all up, and–"

A roar of laughter drowned his words, and Vedder, grabbing up the eel, flung it square at his tormentor. But Frank ducked, and the slimy missile flew past his head to land with a thud on the sand outside. A moment later the sound of taps sent everybody scurrying for his bunk; but for some time after lights were out subdued giggles could be heard from all parts of the camp.

For at least an hour next morning Vedder was very dignified and offish. But he was too easy-going to maintain a grudge very long, and before dinner he had become his comfortable, smiling self again. It was noticed, however, that during the remainder of his stay in camp he pointedly ignored the entire race of snakes, eels, and kindred reptiles.

The athletic meet was a great success. The scouts were divided, according to weight, into juniors and seniors, and there was keen competition in the running, jumping, and swimming events. But great as was the interest excited, it seemed excelled the following afternoon when the crowd set out to resume their hunt for the lost copper-mine. This was both a competition and a fascinating mystery, and a good many beside the members of Tent Three had apparently fallen victims to the spell.

When they reached the starting-point and separated, Ranny and his bunch lost no time in heading for the old foundation. A little digging opened up what seemed to have been the main entrance to the building, but, search as they might, they failed to find anything that in the least resembled a road or path or tramway leading to the mine entrance. Evidently the means by which ore was formerly brought to the smelter had been obliterated by the passing years, and it looked as if they would have to proceed from this point more or less at random.

"It can't be so very far off," said Ranny, as they lined up before him. "We'd better take the hillside first, and remember to look over every foot of ground. The entrance may have been covered by a fall of rock, so we can't count on finding it open. Keep about the same distance apart as you were the other day, and whistle if you strike anything promising."

They set off promptly, Dale Tompkins as before being about the middle of the line, with Court Parker on his right. The thick undergrowth and the rocks piled up in confusion made progress necessarily slow and prevented him from seeing very far in any direction. But every now and then the rustling of bushes or the cracking of dead twigs under foot on either side told Dale that he was keeping on the right course.

For over an hour he searched systematically, zigzagging back and forth along his beat and examining the ground carefully. The slope grew steeper, and at length he paused to wipe the perspiration from his forehead. The sound of foot-falls on his right was plainly audible, and through the undergrowth he glimpsed a khaki-clad figure.

"Say, Court," he called, raising his voice slightly, "found anything yet?"

"It's not Court," came back in Frank Sanson's familiar tones. "What the dickens are you doing so far over, Tommy? Did you change places?"

"Why, no!" Dale's voice was puzzled; instinctively he moved toward the other boy. "I've been keeping right along the way I started," he went on, as they came face to face. "Court was on this side then."

"Sure! He was on my left. I haven't seen him for half an hour or more, but I kept hearing him every now and then. You don't suppose he could have strayed over behind you and to the other side?"

"I don't see how. I'd have heard him, wouldn't I?"

For a moment or so the two boys stood looking at one another in a puzzled fashion. "It's funny," Sanson said at length. "He wouldn't have gone back, either. If he found something, he'd have whistled. Let's call and see if he's over the other way."

Tompkins nodded, and together they walked briskly back a few steps. But it was Ranny Phelps who answered their hail, and in a few moments they saw him coming toward them through the brush.

"What's up?" he asked quickly. "You haven't found–"

"No; it's Court," interrupted Tompkins. "He started out between Frank and me, but he must have got mixed up somehow, for we can't find him. We thought he might be over your way."

"I haven't seen him," said Ranny, briefly. He hesitated an instant and then, pursing up his lips, whistled shrilly. "Best way's to get them all together and straighten things out," he went on. "If he's off his beat, the chances are that part of the ground isn't being looked over at all. This way, fellows."

Bob Gibson was the first to hurry up. Then came Trexler, Bennie Rhead, and lastly Vedder, panting with his haste. But Parker was not among them, nor did Ranny's repeated whistling bring sight or sound of the missing boy. None of the others had seen him since leaving the old foundation, and as they stood there, puzzled and a bit anxious, Tompkins suddenly remembered that for some little time before the meeting with Sanson he had failed to hear the rustlings on his right that had kept him aware of Court's presence. At the time it had seemed unimportant, but now he made haste to mention it.

"Bennie, you chase back to the smelter and see if he's there by any chance," ordered Ranny, crisply, when Dale had finished. "The rest of us get in a close line and beat back along Court's territory. I can't imagine anything happening to him that Tompkins or Sanson wouldn't hear or know about–unless, of course, it's a joke."

His jaw squared in a way that boded ill for the volatile Courtlandt if this should prove to be one of his familiar escapades. But, somehow, Tompkins did not believe that this could be the explanation. Court had been too keenly enthusiastic about the search to delay it by senseless horse-play. Though he, no more than Ranny, could think of any accident which would render the boy unconscious without his making a sound of any sort, Dale took his place in the line with a feeling of distinct uneasiness.

So close together that they could almost touch each other's outstretched hands, the scouts started down the slope. There was little conversation, for by this time all were more or less worried. Just where they expected to find the missing boy would have been hard to tell, but a rabbit could scarcely have escaped their close scrutiny of bush and rock and thorny tangle.

It was fifteen minutes or so before they came to a giant rock that thrust its lichened bulk up from the forest mold. At least that was what it seemed at first–a single, flat-topped mass of stone, ten or twelve feet through and about as high. But passing close to one side, Tompkins and Sanson discovered that it was split in two pieces, one of which had fallen away from the other just enough to leave a jagged crack, not more than three feet wide, between them. A spreading mass of laurel screened the opening from any but the closest inspection, and as he pushed this to one side Dale gave a sudden start and stared intently at the ground beneath it.

"Look at that!" he exclaimed, turning to Frank, who was close behind.

The latter pressed forward and glanced over his shoulder. "What? Oh! You mean– Gee! Didn't you break it off?"

"No!"

Dale's heart was beating unevenly as he bent to pick up the tiny broken twig. There were three leaves on it, as fresh and green as those on the parent bush; the broken end showed white and living. He met Sanson's glance and, dropping the twig, stepped into the jagged crevice. A moment later he gave a smothered cry. At his feet lay a scout hat of brown felt. A few inches beyond yawned a black hole, the leaves and mold and rotten branches about its edges scuffed and torn and freshly broken.

CHAPTER XXV

LOST MINE FOUND

For a long moment the two boys stood motionless, staring wide-eyed and dismayed at the gaping hole before them. Then Dale came to himself with a sudden stiffening of the muscles.

"Get Ranny!" he snapped over his shoulder. And even as the words passed his lips he was conscious of a thrill of thankfulness that the older fellow was here to depend upon. A second later he was stretched out on the ground, his head thrust over the hole.

"Court!" he called loudly. "Court–are you down there?"

For an instant there was no sound. Then his words beat back on him in a queer, sardonic kind of echo that sent a shiver flickering down his spine. He called again, but still there was no reply. Staring down, he tried to penetrate the darkness, but his straining sight could make out nothing but black void. A vivid picture of the mine-shaft he had once seen in Pennsylvania flashed into his mind and turned him cold. Then a step sounded behind him, and lifting his head, he looked into Ranny's set face.

"Does he answer?"

"No."

"Let me get there."

Scrambling to his feet, Dale flattened out against the rock and Ranny took his place. Two or three times the latter shouted Parker's name, but only the echo answered. Then he stood up, and, squeezing past Tompkins, pressed through the crowd of boys gathered about the entrance to the crevice. His face was a little pale, but his jaw was square and he held a scout whistle in one hand. A moment later three long shrill blasts resounded through the woods.

It was the scout danger-signal–a call for help. The boys stood motionless, listening intently for an answer. Presently it came, two short blasts, rather faint and far off, from over the top of the hill.

"That's Mr. Reed, I guess," said Ranny. "I hope he'll bring that coil of rope along. But of course he will. He's not the kind to forget any–"

The words died on his lips; his eyes widened in startled surprise. The others, following the direction of his bewildered gaze, gasped and stared. Bennie Rhead, returned from a fruitless trip to the old foundation, cried out sharply, an undercurrent of fright in his voice.

Around the corner of the great rock Court Parker had stepped quietly into view. He was bareheaded and dirt-streaked, but his face nevertheless wore a broad grin, and after the first shock of surprise had passed, Bob Gibson started forward angrily.

"By heck!" he exclaimed irately. "If you think this sort of thing is funny, Court Parker, it's about time somebody taught you–"

"Shut up, Bob!" cut in Ranny, curtly. His quick eye had taken in the streak of blood on Parker's cheek and noted a slight twitching at the corners of the boy's smiling mouth. "You're not hurt, are you, Court?" he added quickly.

Parker shook his head. "Not to speak of." He drew a long breath. "Well, we've found the mine," he went on in a voice which failed to be quite as matter of fact as he evidently tried to make it.

In an instant he was surrounded by the excited boys and fairly bombarded with questions: "Did you fall down the hole?" "What's it like down there?" "How did you get out?"

Court laughed a little shakily and sat down suddenly on a rock. "Give me a chance, can't you?" he begged. "I've only got one tongue, even though I can make that go pretty fast."

"Cut it out and quit worrying him, fellows," ordered Ranny. "Take your time, Court, and start at the beginning. How did you get down the hole?"

"Cinchiest thing you know!" grinned Parker. "I just stepped on the cover and went through. You see, when I went into that crack the hole didn't show at all; there were a lot of branches and stuff over it. One minute I was on solid ground, and the next I was flying through space."

"Gee!" exclaimed Sanson. "How deep was it?"

"Seemed about a mile; but I guess it wasn't more than twenty feet. Luckily there was a lot of leaves and stuff at the bottom, so I landed pretty soft. But when I tried to climb back I found it was too slippery. Then I lost my voice yelling, but nobody came, so I started to look around a bit. It's just one long tunnel, running both ways and braced up by rotten old timbers and things. I had my flash-light in my pocket, so I wasn't afraid of being lost. I took the right-hand turn and–I say, fellows, there's a bear down there!"

"A bear?" chorused the astonished audience as one boy.

In an instant he was surrounded by excited boys

"Well, it might be a wildcat or something like that. I only saw its eyes, but I tell you they held me up, all right. About three hundred feet from where I fell in there was another kind of a shaft thing, only not so big, sort of off to one side. It wasn't very deep, either, for when I looked down I saw those two big yellow eyes that didn't seem more than eight or ten feet down. Gee whiz! I was scared. I must have got turned around, too; because, when I came to, I found I was legging it away from the big hole instead of back toward it."

He paused and drew a long breath; his fascinated hearers sighed in sympathy. "Did you go back then?" one of them asked eagerly.

"I was thinking about it," resumed Court, "when my thumb slipped off the flash-key, and ahead of me, not so very far away, was a little spot of light–daylight, you know. You'd better believe I hustled for it. The tunnel had been going up hill quite some, and now it began to get narrower and lower. Before very long I had to get down and crawl, and then I found the light was coming between two rocks through a crack that didn't look more than a foot or so wide. The bottom was pounded down hard in a regular path; I s'pose that was the way the bear got in to its den. Anyhow, there was just room for me to squeeze out, and even then I cut my face and tore these holes in my suit."

"Kind of small, then, for a full-grown bear, I should think," commented Ranny.

Court looked a trifle foolish. "I never thought of that," he confessed. "Still, I bet a wildcat could do it."

"It might–only I haven't heard of any wild-cats being around here."

"What's the matter with our taking a look?" suggested Dale Tompkins.

"Going through the hole Court came out of?" asked Ranny, glancing at him.

"Sure! We've got some flash-lights, and very likely the beast is stuck down that shaft and can't get out. I vote we try it."

Two or three fellows backed him up, but the others showed no great enthusiasm in the venture. They were quite willing, however, to go as far as the outside of the hole, and started off without delay, only to meet Mr. Reed with Mr. Curtis and several scouts coming up at a brisk trot.

When Court's story had been told over again the scoutmasters decided that the investigation had better be made from the end that Court had stumbled into. They had brought the rope with them, and when one end of this was firmly fastened, Mr. Reed slid down into the old mine. He spent some time inspecting the ancient timbering, but finally decided that it was safe enough for those who wished to follow him. This meant the entire assembled crowd, and when all were gathered at the bottom, Court led the way.

The tunnel was fairly wide and over six feet high. It sloped gently upward and was quite dry, thus accounting for the preservation of the massive oak beams that acted as supports. Here and there along the sides were the marks of tools, but scarcely a vestige of ore remained.

"Vein petered out, I suppose," remarked Mr. Curtis. "That's why it was abandoned, of course."

The interest of the scouts, however, was less on the mine than on Court's "wildcat." As they approached the shaft some hurried forward while others kept prudently in the rear.

"He's there yet!" announced Parker, peering over the edge. "See his eyes! I wonder if–"

He did not finish. Mr. Reed flashed the light from his battery into the hole, and Trexler, close beside him, gave an exclamation of surprise.

"Why, it's a coon!"

And so it was; an uncommonly large specimen, to be sure, but still exceedingly harmless and inoffensive. In fact, at the flashes of light and the sight of so many faces peering down on it, the frightened creature shrank close to the side of the pit as if trying to escape.

"It's fallen down and can't get out!" exclaimed Trexler. "Can't I go down and get it, Mr. Reed?"

The hole was barely four feet across and not more than twice as deep–a trial shaft, Mr. Curtis suggested, probably sunk in the search for another vein. Receiving permission, Paul simply hung by his hands and dropped, and the interested spectators saw him lift up the coon.

"The poor thing's half starved," he said. "Let down a couple of coats, fellows, and pull him up. He'll make a dandy camp mascot."

The idea was hailed with delight. There was little trouble in hoisting the creature to the surface and pulling Trexler after him. Then the entire crowd turned back to the entrance shaft, their interest diverted to this new pet.

Back on the surface the assembly whistle was blown, and the two scoutmasters made themselves comfortable while waiting the arrival of the throng they knew would be eager to inspect the mine. The members of Tent Three, however, did not linger. Obtaining permission to return at once to camp, they hustled off, carrying the coon with them, and for the brief remainder of the day they were exceedingly busy.

Pete, as the mascot was christened, had to be fed and housed and cared for, and it took some time to build a crate strong enough to keep him from escaping. At first he threatened to be killed by kindness, but finally Trexler was voted his special guardian, and in a surprisingly short time the animal became noticeably docile and friendly. He had an inordinate curiosity and was as full of mischief as any monkey. But though the cook frowned on him, his popularity with the scouts increased with every day.

CHAPTER XXVI

THE WISH OF HIS HEART

And how swiftly those remaining days passed with their mingling of work and play! There were more fishing excursions and athletic meets. One afternoon was devoted to an exciting treasure-hunt; another saw a sham battle in which part of the boys in boats attacked one of the islands defended by the remainder. At regular intervals, too, Captain Chalmers gave scout examinations in headquarters tent, and an encouraging number of fellows increased their standing or obtained merit badges.

Dale Tompkins thoroughly enjoyed each minute of his stay. He entered with keen zest into every game and competition, and took his share of the various chores–even the hated dish-washing–without a grumble. It was all so fresh and wonderful that the simplicity and freedom of the life, with the nightly council-fire under the stars and the intimate companionship with so many "dandy" fellows, appealed to him intensely even without considering the added interest of each day's activities.

Best of all, perhaps, was his feeling of growing comfort in the attitude of Ranny Phelps. There had been nothing in the nature of a formal reconciliation. On the contrary, the blond lad's manner toward Tompkins still showed traces of embarrassment. But one does not always need the spoken word to realize the truth, and deep down in his heart Dale knew that, though they might not yet be close friends, at least no shadow of coldness or enmity remained between them.

When the last day came, as last days have an unpleasant way of doing, Dale tried to think of the wonderful time he had had instead of regretting that it was almost over. More than once, too, his mind dwelt with gratitude on the unknown customer whose need for bird-houses had made it all possible.

"Maybe some day I'll find out who it was and be able to thank him," he said to himself during the course of the morning.

A final trip in the motor-boat had been planned for the afternoon, but after dinner Captain Chalmers announced that Mr. Thornton would inspect the camp at about five o'clock, and stay for supper and the council-fire afterward.

"So I think we'd better put in a few hours making things spick and span and working up a specially good program for to-night," he concluded. "You fellows all know how keen I am to give him an extra good impression of scouting, and you've kept things in corking good shape these two weeks. But let's see if we can't give him a regular knock-out blow when he comes."

One and all the scouts took up the idea enthusiastically and worked to such purpose that when the banker appeared he found a camp which would have done credit to the West Point cadets. He was a little stiff at first, but during supper in the big tent he thawed considerably, and later, at the council-fire, he applauded the various stunts with the enjoyment and simple abandon, almost, of a boy. When these were over he rose to his feet, and the firelight gleaming on his face showed it softened into lines of genial good-fellowship.

"I've had a mighty good time to-night, boys," he said, glancing around the circle of eager, young faces. "I just want to thank you for it and tell you frankly that what I've seen of Hillsgrove Boy Scouts has changed my mind completely about the whole proposition. If you fellows are a fair sample of scouting generally,–as I begin to suspect you are,–I see no reason why you should not consider this camp a permanent thing, to come back to every year and be responsible for and do with as you like. I should very much–"

The wild yell of delight which went up drowned the remainder of his remarks. Leaping to his feet, MacIlvaine called for a cheer, and the three times three, with a tiger at the end, was given with a vigor that left no doubt of the boys' feelings. When comparative quiet was restored Mr. Thornton thanked them briefly and said he would like to shake hands with every one of the scouts present.

Laughing and jostling, the boys formed in line, and as each paused before the banker, Captain Chalmers introduced him. Tompkins was just behind Ranny, and he could not fail to notice the extra vigor Mr. Thornton put into his handshake.

"I'm very glad to meet you, Phelps," he said genially. "Your father and I are old friends. In fact, I dined with him at Hillsgrove only a few days ago. And by the way, I was immensely taken with those bird-houses on the place and want some like them for my own. He told me you had put them around just before you came down here. Did you make them yourself?"

The usually self-contained Ranleigh turned crimson and dropped his eyes. "N-no, sir," he stammered. "They were made by–by–another–I'll write the address down, and–and give it to you afterward."

He passed on, and the boy behind him took his place. In a daze Dale felt his hand shaken and heard the sound of Mr. Thornton's pleasant voice, but the words were as meaningless as if they had been spoken in another tongue. Muttering some vague reply, he dropped the other's hand and was swept on by the crowd behind.

Out of the whirling turmoil of his mind one thing alone stood forth sharply. Those were his bird-houses; they could not possibly be any other. It was Ranny who had given him these wonderful two weeks–Ranny, whom he thought–

His head went up suddenly and, glancing around, he caught sight of the blond chap disappearing toward the beach. In a few moments he was at his side.

"Ranny!" he exclaimed impulsively. "You–you–"

Something gripped his throat, making further speech impossible. Phelps stirred uneasily.

"Well," he said with a touch of defiance, "I wanted them, and–and I couldn't make them myself. I–I'm a perfect dub with tools."

"You–you did it to–give me a chance at camp."

Dale's voice was strained and uneven. His hand still rested on the other's arm, and in the brief silence that followed he felt Ranny stiffen a little.

"Ranny!" he exclaimed impulsively. "You–you–"

"If I did, it was only fair," the older chap said suddenly, in low, abrupt tones. "I–I've been a beastly cad, Dale. I've worked against you every way I could." His voice grew sharp and self-reproachful. "I kept it up like a stubborn mule even when I began to see– Why, look at the rotten, conceited way I kept you out of baseball. After that it was only–decent to do what I could to–make up."

They stood in the moonlight, the water at their feet, while back among the trees the fire blazed up, sending a shower of sparks drifting across the spangled heavens. The talk and laughter of the crowd gathered there seemed to come from very far away.

"You did it to–to square up, then?" Dale asked presently in a low tone.

There was another pause. Suddenly an arm slid about his shoulders, and for the first time Ranny turned and looked him squarely in the eyes.

"No," he answered quietly. "It was because I wanted us to be in camp–together."

CHAPTER XXVII

THE SURPRISE

The last barrier of reserve between the two had fallen. From that moment they were friends of the sort Dale had sometimes dreamed of, but only lately dared to hope for. And as the weeks lengthened into months, as summer sped along to fall, the bond grew closer, until they became well-nigh inseparable. In school and out, on the football field, at scout meetings, on hikes, they were always together, until at last those early days of clash and bitterness seemed as unreal as the figments of a dream.

Troop Five held well together during the following winter. Inevitably, two or three boys dropped out and new ones took their places. But the majority stayed on and had better times than ever on the lake and in their cabin. After Christmas they began work in earnest on their share of the big scout rally, which was to be given in the spring to illustrate for the towns-people the aims and purposes of scouting, and also as a means of gaining new recruits. Every troop was to take part, and not a little good-natured rivalry developed between them.

Troop Five was to illustrate the various uses of the scout staff in a number of drills and formations, the most effective and also the most difficult of which was one that Mr. Curtis called the riot wedge. Though necessitating a good deal of hard work, most of the boys were keen about it, for they were determined to excel the work of the other troops. Perhaps the only fellow who complained was only Bob Gibson, and he wouldn't have seemed himself at all without finding something to grumble about.

"Gee! but I'm sick of this silly drill!" he growled under his breath one night when they had been practising steadily for an hour. He slumped his shoulders a bit and his staff tilted to a slovenly angle. "What's the sense of it, anyhow?"

"'Tention!" rang out the quick, decisive voice of Scoutmaster Curtis, standing slim and erect before the line of scouts. "We'll try that once more, fellows, and get a little snap into it this time. Bob, if you could manage to support your staff in an upright position, it would improve the looks of the line."

There was no sting in his tone, and Bob, grinning sheepishly, straightened his shoulders and brought his staff to the same angle as the others.

"Prepare to form riot wedge!" ordered the scoutmaster, crisply. "One!"

There was a rapid thud of feet and a swift, scurrying movement which might have seemed to the uninitiated meaningless and without purpose. But when the stir had ceased and silence fell, each of the three patrols had formed itself into a regular wedge with one of the largest, strongest boys at the apex and the patrol-leader standing in the middle of the base. Their staves were upright, but at the sharp command of "Two!" these swung into a horizontal position, the ends crossing and the whole becoming a continuous barrier with the boys behind it.

"Fine and dandy!" approved Mr. Curtis. "That's more the way it ought to go. Now, let's try the double wedge I showed you last week. Eagle patrol, dress a little to the left; Beavers to the right. Ready? One!"

This time there was a little more confusion, for the movement was newer and more complicated than the other. Raven patrol took position as before, though spreading out a bit and gathering in a boy from each of the other patrols to form the ends of the larger wedge. The Eagle and Beaver patrols then swung around against either side of the wedge, each boy covering the space between the two lads behind him. The final manœuver thus presented a double row of scouts linked together by their lowered staves into a formation that would be equally effective in pushing through a dense crowd or withstanding the pressure of their assaults.

"Good!" smiled Mr. Curtis. "A bit slow, of course, but we'll get it all right. Now, fellows, I'd like to have a full attendance next week. Captain Chalmers will address the troop on a special matter, and I think by that time I'll have a rather pleasant surprise for you. Has any one any questions to ask before we break up?"

Court Parker saluted, his face serious save for an irrepressible twinkle in his eyes. "Couldn't you–er–tell us about the surprise to-night, sir?" he asked. "Next week's an awful long time off, you know."

The scoutmaster smiled. "You'll enjoy it all the more when it comes," he returned. "Besides, it isn't quite ready to be told yet. I think that's all to-night, fellows. Patrol-leaders dismiss their patrols."

As the crowd poured out of the building a chorus of eager speculation arose.

"Wonder if it's anything to do with camp," suggested Frank Sanson.

"How could it be?" objected Dale Tompkins, his arm across Ranny Phelps's shoulder. "Camp couldn't be much better than it was last summer; and if he's had word we can't use the place–well, that wouldn't be exactly pleasant."

"Right, old scout!" approved Ranny. Then his face grew suddenly serious. "Do you suppose it could be about–the war?" he ventured.

There was a momentary silence. In Hillsgrove, as in most other parts of the country, war and rumors of war had been plentiful of late. The ruthless German submarine campaign had been on for weeks. Only a few days before, the severing of diplomatic relations with that government had made a great stir. Everywhere people were wondering what would be the next step, and, according to temperament or conviction, were complaining of governmental sloth or praising the President's diplomacy. In all of this the boys had naturally taken more or less part, wondering, speculating, planning–a little spectacularly, perhaps–what they would do if war actually came.

Suddenly Bob Gibson sniffed. "Shucks!" he commented dogmatically. "Of course it isn't. I don't believe in this war business. I'll bet that old surprise is some silly thing not worth mentioning. I'll bet it's as foolish as the riot wedge. If anybody can tell me what good that is or ever would be, I'll give him an ice-cream soda. When would there ever be a riot in this one-horse burg? I'd like to know. And if there was one, what would a bunch of fellows like us be able to do against–"

"Oh, cut it out!" begged Ranny Phelps. "You know you're just talking to hear the sound of your own voice."

"Am not!" growled Gibson, stubbornly. "Here we've wasted over an hour on the blooming thing, and it's not the first time, either, he's kept us late. It's getting to be nothing but drill, drill, drill, and it makes me sick."

"Don't be an idiot just because you happen to know how," urged Ranny, a touch of earnestness beneath his banter. "You know perfectly well it isn't all drill, or anything like it. Maybe there's been more of it just lately, but I don't see any sense in taking up a thing unless you do it right. Trouble with you, Bob, you're so set and stubborn that you've got to find something to kick about or argue against or you wouldn't be happy. I'll bet if Dan Beard himself came out for a talk, you'd want to give him points on camping, or forestry, or something like that."

There was a shout of laughter from the others that brought a touch of color to Gibson's cheeks. He growled out an emphatic denial, but Ranny had hit the mark so accurately that Bob dropped the subject for the time.

There was not a vacant place in the line the next Monday, and when the scout commissioner stepped forward to speak he was greeted with flattering attention. Some of this was due to his position in the movement; but a great deal more, it must be confessed arose from the fact that he was an exceedingly active and competent officer in the national guard, and as such was regarded by the boys as a rather superior being.

"I've only a few words to say, fellows," Captain Chalmers began. "From now on I want you all to work extra hard on your signaling and first aid. These are the two features of scouting which, in the near future, may be particularly valuable. Keep up your practice for the rally, but give all the rest of your spare time to these two things. There's one more point. How many of you would like to learn something of the regular military drill? Those interested, step forward one pace."

With a swift movement the whole line swayed forward. Captain Chalmers nodded approvingly.

"Fine!" he said. "I want to make this another feature of the rally. With your permission, Mr. Curtis, I'll start them in on the rudiments to-night. The staves, of course, will take the place of arms."

The hour which followed seemed one of the briefest the boys had ever known. The captain was no easy taskmaster, but not even Bob Gibson grumbled. There was something inspiring in those snappy, authoritative orders, in the rhythmic tramp of marching feet, in the growing sense of efficiency and pride with each movement understood and properly executed. Every one of the twenty-four scouts put his whole being into the work, and in the end they were rewarded by Captain Chalmers's pleased approval.

"That's great!" he said when at length they stood at ease. "I didn't think you'd do so well. Keep it up in that spirit, and we'll all be proud of you. After this, Mr. Curtis will do the drilling. Besides practising what you've already learned, one new evolution thoroughly mastered at each meeting will be about all you ought to undertake."

He stepped back, and Mr. Curtis took his place. At the sight of the folded paper in his hand a sudden ripple of interest ran down the line.

"Gee!" muttered Frank Sanson. "I'd forgotten all about the surprise!"

"I have a letter here from Mr. Thornton, fellows," said the scoutmaster, unfolding the paper. Smiling a little, his glance ranged over the long line of eager, inquiring faces; then it dropped to the sheet before him, and he read aloud slowly:

"My dear Curtis:

"As you know from my note of ten days or more ago, I have amused myself during the past few months by having a permanent mess-shack and recreation-room built on the site of the big dining-tent. The finishing touches will be put to this within a few days, and I think something in the nature of a housewarming is in order. It will give me great pleasure if your troop can be my guests down at the camp during their Easter vacation, which begins, I understand, toward the last of the month. By that time the weather ought to be mild enough for a week of tent life–at least for Boy Scouts; and there will always be the new building to fall back on. I will see to the transportation back and forth, and I hope every one of your boys will be able to come.

"Sincerely yours,

"John Thornton."

For an instant there was a dazed silence throughout the room. Then a yell broke forth which could have been heard–and was–as far as the green. Breaking ranks, boys clutched one another in exuberant embraces and pranced madly about the hall. Then there was more shouting, and throwing-up of hats, and general disorder, which Mr. Curtis made no attempt to check. When failing breath brought comparative quiet, he raised his hand for silence.

"I gather that the invitation meets with your approval," he remarked with a smile. "Shall I send Mr. Thornton the grateful acceptance of the whole troop?"

"You bet!" came back promptly and emphatically from a dozen voices. "Wough! He's some good sport!" "Think of it, fellows! A new mess-shack! A whole week in camp in April!" "Pinch me, somebody; I don't believe I'm awake at all!"

The last speaker was promptly accommodated, and after a little additional skylarking, things quieted down. Before the meeting broke up, Mr. Curtis wrote a letter of sincere thanks and acceptance to John Thornton, which each one of the scouts signed with a flourish. After that, with youthful inconsequence, they hustled home to obtain parental sanction.

CHAPTER XXVIII

WAR!

In some miraculous fashion the necessary permission was obtained by each and every one of the boys of Troop Five, and bright and early on the morning after school closed the whole crowd was packed into the motor-truck, jouncing southward over roads very much the worse for spring thaws. It was, in fact, a vastly more uncomfortable trip than the one last summer. But overhead the skies were cloudless; warm breezes, faintly odorous of spring and growing things, caressed their cheeks, and youth was in their hearts. What cared they for hard seats, for jolts and jounces, for mud-holes, delays, and the growing certainty of a late arrival? A thrilling week, golden with possibilities, lay before them, and nothing else mattered. They chattered and sang and ate, and stopped by wayside springs, and ate again. The sun was setting when they lumbered into Clam Cove and tumbled out of the truck to find the old Aquita waiting at the landing. Then came the chugging passage of the bay, and the landing at the new dock they had not even heard of, but where they did not pause long, so eager were they all to inspect the mess-shack, bulking large and unfamiliar through the gathering dusk.

It wasn't really a shack at all, but a commodious log structure some forty feet by twenty–big, airy, and spacious. There were benches and tables of rough yet solid construction, bracket-lamps, many windows, and a cavernous stone fireplace in which a roaring blaze of logs leaped and crackled. The size and scale of it all fairly awed the boys, and they stared eagerly around for Mr. Thornton. To their disappointment the banker was not to be seen.

"He had to go to Washington unexpected," explained the man in charge to Mr. Curtis. "But he sent word you was to make yourselves at home, and he'd be back just as soon as he could."

This put a momentary damper on the affair, but it was not of long duration. There was too much to see and do in the short time at their disposal for regrets of any sort. There was little accomplished that night, however. After a hearty supper, beds were made up on the floor and every one was glad to turn in early.

They were up with the sun, and then began a strenuous period of mingled work and play which filled to overflowing each waking hour of the three days that followed. They got out the tents and erected them in the old places. They took hikes and motor-boat trips; they fished and explored, talked to each other with signal-flags, and put in a commendable amount of time on their drill. They were so constantly employed extracting the last atom of enjoyment from the brief vacation that they quite failed to notice the slight abstraction of their scoutmaster, or the manner in which he watched the mails and fairly devoured the daily paper. Not one of them found time even to glance at that paper himself, much less think of, or discuss the affairs of the nation and the world. Then, suddenly, came the awakening.

It was toward noon on the fourth day of their stay–a Tuesday; they remembered that afterward. The crowd had been for a hike to Lost Mine, and, returning, had dawdled lazily, for the air was almost oppressively balmy. Dale, Ranny, and Court Parker were considerably ahead of the others, and as they reached the parade-ground they came suddenly upon Harry Vedder, whose turn it had been to fetch the mail and paper. The plump boy's face was flushed and moist; his expression fairly exuded importance.

"Well!" he stated, without waiting for them to speak. "It's come."

Ranny stared. "Come?" he repeated. "What are you talking about, Dumpling? What's come?"

Vedder puffed out his fat cheeks. "War!" he said solemnly.

For an instant no one spoke. Dale felt a queer, tingling thrill go through him. The thing seemed unreal, impossible. Somehow these past few weeks of delay and hesitation had thrust the idea farther and farther into the background of his mind. He caught a glimpse of Parker's face, dazed and incredulous.

"What!" gasped Ranny. "You mean with–"

"Yep," nodded Vedder. "The President made a fine speech last night to Congress, or something. I heard 'em talking about it at the post-office. Everybody's as excited as the dickens. I guess it's in all the papers, too, only Mr. Curtis's wasn't open."

Dale's eyes sought headquarters tent. Under the rolled-up flap he could see the scoutmaster sitting on his cot, his head bent intently over an outspread paper. Again that curious tingling went through the boy. Behind him the shouts and laughter of the approaching crowd seemed suddenly incongruous and out of place. He glanced again at Vedder, whose round face still radiated self-importance, and wondered how the boy could look so smug and complacent.

"Did Congress declare war?" asked Ranny, abruptly.

"I dunno; I guess so. They're going to raise a whopping army. I heard one man say everybody from nineteen to twenty-five would have to go."

"Have to go!" shrilled Court Parker. "Why, they'll want to go, won't they? I wish I was more than sixteen."

Unconsciously the four were moving toward the scoutmaster's tent. Others, hearing a word or two, caught up with them, and the news was passed quickly along. The throng paused at the tent entrance. Dale caught a glimpse of the newspaper across the top of which flared in black capitals:

PRESIDENT CALLS FOR WAR DECLARATION

"It's true, then, Mr. Curtis!" Ranny Phelps exclaimed. "I thought it was coming. When are they going to–"

"Hold your horses, Ranny," interrupted the scoutmaster. He stood up and came toward them, his face curiously elated. "There's no time to answer a lot of questions now. Mess-call will sound any time. Hustle and wash up, fellows, and after dinner we'll talk this over."

Curious and excited as they were, no one protested. They scattered to their tents, chattering volubly, and the mess-call found them still speculating and asking questions of one another. During the meal the discussion continued but in a slightly more subdued key. A state of things which at first had seemed merely exciting and soul-stirring was coming home more keenly. They were beginning to make individual applications. Captain Chalmers would be called out, of course. Though over thirty, Mr. Curtis himself might enlist. Then some one thought suddenly of Wesley Becker, who was just nineteen. That seemed the strangest thing of all, for Wes, despite his semi-leadership, was merely one of themselves. But of course it was all the merest speculation; they didn't really know anything yet. So when the meal was over and Mr. Curtis rose slowly in his place, there was a long, concerted sigh of relaxing tension.

"Fellows," began the scoutmaster, quietly, "I want to read you the President's message delivered to Congress last night. You won't find it dull. On the contrary it's about the most vivid, vital piece of writing I have ever read. It puts clearly before us the situation we are facing. It will make you prouder than ever of your country and its head."

And without further preamble he began to read that wonderful document which has stirred the world and has taken its place among the immortal utterances of men. And as he read, eyes brightened, boyish faces flushed, brown hands gripped the rough edges of bench or table, or strained tightly over clasped knees. He finished, and there came a brief, eloquent moment of utter silence, followed by a swift outburst of wild applause.

The scoutmaster's face lit up with a smile. "It's great, isn't it?" he said. "Makes you feel mighty proud to have a man like that at the helm." He folded the paper and laid it on the table before him. "And now," he went on, his shoulders squaring a bit, "I want to say a few words myself. A state of war exists, for Congress cannot help but back up the man who wrote that message. It's been coming for a long time. Many of us have felt it and tried to plan a little in advance. Your signaling and first aid and drilling have all been with that idea in view. What I want now is that you shall give more time than ever to those things–practically all the rest of your time in camp here. Remember George Lancaster, that English chap who was in Troop One several years ago. To-day he's one of the best signalers in the British army. It will mean hard work, but, unless I'm far wrong, work will swiftly come to be the great slogan throughout the country. Will you do this, fellows? Stand up, every one who's willing."

There was a rush, a clatter–a bench was overturned–in ten seconds not a boy remained seated.

"Fine!" smiled Mr. Curtis. "I thought I could count on you. When Mr. Thornton comes on Friday we'll show him something that will surprise him. And we'll give those folks at the rally something to think about, too."

"But are we still going to have the rally, sir?" asked Bob Gibson.

Mr. Curtis laughed. "Of course we are," he said emphatically. "You mustn't think, Bob, that a state of war is going to disrupt the entire country. That would be hysterical. There'll be unusual doings, of course. Things will be a bit different in many ways. But school and chores and all the ordinary routine of your daily lives must go on as they always have. Suppose we get out now and work up a little program for Mr. Thornton's benefit."

The days that followed, so radically different from anything the boys had planned, showed up their spirit admirably. Of course there were grumblers; those develop in any situation where discipline is involved. There were many moments of weariness and discouragement, too, when it seemed as if proficiency could never be attained. But underneath it all, stirring, invigorating, that wonderful sense of service–service to another, service to their country, perhaps, upheld and strengthened them. What they were doing was not merely play. Some day or other, far away or near, it would be of value; and the measure of that value no man could tell.

Mr. Thornton was due to reach camp Friday afternoon. The Aquita, in charge of Wesley Becker and another scout, went over to meet him, and as soon as the motor-boat was seen returning, a bugle blast summoned the others hastily from their tents.

"Fall in!" ordered Mr. Curtis, crisply. "Phelps will take charge while I go down to the dock."

Only their eyes moved, but these followed him to the landing and they saw Mr. Thornton step ashore and pause for a moment or two of conversation before heading for the parade-ground. The banker's face looked tired and his shoulders drooped a little. But as he caught sight of the scouts drawn up in a straight, soldierly line behind the colors his head went up and his eyes brightened with surprise and interest.

"'Tention, troop!" called Mr, Curtis, sharply. "Right dress!–Front!–Present arms!"

The "arms" were, of course, their staves, but the manœuver was executed with a snap and precision which many a company of militia might have envied. Then came the command, "Count off!" followed by, "Fours left–march!" and the squad swung smartly down the parade-ground.

In the half-hour of manœuvering which followed–and this included some fairly difficult formations for new recruits–every boy gave the best that was in him. And when it was all over, the expression on Mr. Thornton's face was quite reward enough. At the command, "Fall out!" they surged around him, shaking him by the hand, thanking him exuberantly, and all trying at once to tell him how much more wonderful everything was than they had expected.

The council-fire that night was built out on the point instead of in the great stone fireplace. Because of Mr. Thornton's presence, a special program had been arranged. There were scout games and stunts in abundance, songs galore, and a number of other features which had proved effective last summer. But it wasn't quite all gaiety and careless amusement. Mingling with the joking and laughter and occasional bit of skylarking was a touch of sober seriousness. It was their last night in camp together. Moreover, from that momentous Tuesday things had never been really quite the same. Their daily drills and practice were rousing in them a sense of responsibility. They knew that all over the country preparations for war were being pushed energetically. There had been time also, to hear from home–of how this brother talked of enlisting in the marines, or that cousin, a member of Captain Chalmers's own regiment, who had been ordered to hold himself in readiness to join the colors. And so at the end, standing shoulder to shoulder around the blaze, their young voices ringing out in the stirring strains of "America," more than one throat tightened, and there were few who did not feel a tingling thrill beyond the thrill those verses usually evoked.

There came a pause. Then slowly John Thornton rose and stood for a moment facing them in silence.

"I want to thank you, boys," he said at length, in tones which emotion had rendered brusk and almost harsh. "It–it has been a privilege and more than pleasure to see your surprising work this afternoon and to be with you in this way to-night. I am proud of you–prouder than you can ever know. I can say nothing more than this," and his voice rang out suddenly with a note that stirred them inexplicably: "If only the youth of our country will measure up to your standards in the crisis that is before us, we need fear nothing for the future."

CHAPTER XXIX

"EVERY SCOUT TO FEED A SOLDIER"

The returning scouts found Hillsgrove buzzing with preparation. In fact, so changed was the atmosphere of the town that it was hard to believe they had been away for little more than a week. Several of the young men had already enlisted in army or navy. The post-office, courthouse, and many of the stores displayed inspiring posters urging others to do the same. A home guard was being organized for the purpose of dealing effectually with any sort of disturbance from resident foreigners, while a number of men, both young and middle-aged, talked of forming a regular military troop to be drilled twice weekly on the green by army officers or men who had been at Plattsburg.

It was all stirring and inspiring, and there is no telling to what extent the members of Troop Five might have become involved had not Mr. Curtis given them a serious talk at the first meeting after their return from camp. Captain Chalmers had departed with his regiment to take up guard duty along the line in one of the important railroads of the State, leaving Mr. Curtis in general charge of the scout situation at Hillsgrove; so that this talk was later repeated in substance at meetings of the other troops.

"I know you're all very keen to get into things and do your bit," he said, when the boys gathered around him in the parish-house. "The only question, of course, is how you can be most useful without frittering away your time. I've taken the matter up with headquarters, and talked it over with the mayor and several other men, and have come to this conclusion: first of all, we'll go ahead with our preparations for the rally, but instead of having it a free exhibition, as we planned, we'll charge admission and turn over the proceeds to the Red Cross. Next, I'm going to organize a signaling corps and a first-aid division formed of the real experts in each troop. There may be no immediate use for either of these, but you'll be ready when the time comes. Then there is the detail of helping to keep public order, in which the Boy Scouts have always been especially useful. There is no telling when or where you may be called upon, but your training and discipline helps you to quick thinking and action."

He paused an instant, and then his voice took on a deeper, more earnest note. "But more important than anything else just now is the need for each one of you to do everything in his power to help conserve and increase the food supply. All over the world this supply is low. The whole of Europe looks to us for a goodly proportion of its daily bread, and we've got to meet that expectation. We've got to make this a year of bumper crops, even at a time when labor will naturally be scarcer than ever. And to help out in this crisis the men at the head of the Boy Scout movement have adopted a motto–a slogan–which should be first and foremost in every scout's mind until the war is over. 'Every Scout to Feed a Soldier!' Isn't that fine? A scout with a hoe may equal a man with a gun. The President himself has stated more than once that a man may serve his country as effectually in the corn-field as at the front. And how much more is this the duty of a boy whose age makes it impossible for him to reach the firing-line. I've known you fellows too long and too intimately to have any doubts as to your responses to this appeal. Those of you who have home gardens that will take all your time must look after them, releasing, if possible, some man for other work. The others, I hope, will volunteer their services to any one needing them, and I expect very soon to have an organized clearing-house for farmers in the neighborhood needing help and boys willing to furnish it. I may say that any one going into this will be allowed to absent himself from the afternoon school session and all day on Wednesdays. Later, the schools may be closed entirely for workers. Now, I know this doesn't sound nearly so stirring and patriotic as joining a military company and drilling and all that; but this isn't a moment in which to pick and choose. The duty of each one of us is to give himself where he is most needed. And, believe me, fellows, by helping to plant and harvest you will be performing the highest sort of service to your country and humanity. I want you to think this over to-night, and from to-morrow on I'll be ready to take the names of volunteers."

It was a rather silent crowd that filed out of the meeting-room a little later. To the great majority Mr. Curtis's proposition certainly didn't sound in the least interesting or alluring. On the contrary it had a decidedly depressing effect, and several openly declared that they'd be hanged if they'd spend the entire summer in that kind of drudgery. But second thought, aided, perhaps, by a little solid advice at home, wrought a change. The next afternoon the fellows held a private meeting of their own at which the few persistent objectors were crushed by bodily force, when necessary, and which ended in the whole troop volunteering as a body.

It wasn't at all an easy thing for some of them to do. In boys like Ranny Phelps, who loathed "grubbing with a hoe" and had never had the slightest experience in farming, it was something almost akin to heroism. But not one of them shirked or backed down. Within a week they were all placed, and, from that time on, blistered hands, weary backs, and aching muscles were the order of the day. As Ranny once expressed it,–airily, but with an underlying touch of seriousness,–the only bright spots in the week were Sunday, when they could sleep late, and the two afternoons they were let off at four o'clock to practise for the rally.

They made the most of those brief hours. In good weather the drill took place in a pasture belonging to old Mr. Grimstone, after which they enjoyed a refreshing plunge in the lake, and generally ended up with supper in the cabin. When he had time, which wasn't often, Mr. Curtis joined them. Usually Ranny Phelps was in charge, and whenever they could they carried off Mr. Grimstone for supper.

It was on one of these latter occasions, as they sat out on the bank of the lake after supper, that Frank Sanson suddenly voiced a feeling which was present, more or less often, in the breast of every scout in the troop.

"Mr. Grimstone," he said abruptly, "I don't suppose you realize what a dandy thing you did when you gave us this place. I don't know what we'd do without it now; do you, fellows?"

There was an emphatic chorus of agreement which brought a touch of color into the old man's leathery, tanned face and made him shuffle his feet uneasily. Then suddenly he raised his eyes and there was a twinkle in them.

"It ain't me you ought to thank," he said abruptly. "It's that Dale boy there; he's to blame."

"Dale Tompkins!" exclaimed several surprised voices at once. "Why, what's he got to do with it?"

"Most everything," returned Grimstone, briefly. "It was him that brought out my dinner last Thanksgivin', an cooked it, an' et it with me. That's what give me a new idea of you boys, an' nothin' else."

An astonished silence followed, broken presently by a low whistle from Mr. Curtis. "Well, what do you know about that," he murmured. "A good turn come home to roost!"

But no one heard him, for the whole crowd, as one boy, had pounced on Tompkins and was pummeling him and rolling him about over the ground to the accompaniment of shouts and laughter and jocular, approving comment.

Glancing sidewise at Caleb Grimstone, the scoutmaster's eyes widened with surprise and sudden comprehension. The old man's gaze was fixed on the flushed, laughing face of the kicking, protesting victim. His own brown face glowed; his stern, tight lips were relaxed in a smile which was almost tender.

CHAPTER XXX

THE SILVER CROSS

In spite of their long and careful preparation, the members of Troop Five were not a little keyed up and excited when the night of the big scout rally finally arrived. Each boy dressed with unusual care, and the majority reached the parish-house some time before the hour named for assembling. From here they marched in good order to the old-fashioned frame building, whose entire third floor constituted the masonic hall, where the performance was to come off. Another troop was close on their heels, and, in their hurry to get there first, the boys pushed and jostled one another on the narrow, twisting stairs. But in the hallway above they paused to fall in, and at the word of command from Mr. Curtis they marched through the double doors into the brightly lighted assembly-room, wheeled smartly to the right, and took up their position at one side of the doorway.

The hall was already well filled and resounded with the buzz of conversation. Pretty girls in Red Cross costumes flitted among the audience seeking contributions and memberships. By eight o'clock the rows of chairs that packed over half the big room were occupied, and there were people standing. When the doors were finally closed and the entertainment began, the place was almost uncomfortably jammed by a throng of proud mothers and fathers and brothers and sisters of the performers, to say nothing of a great many other members of the community who were interested in the movement or curious to see the result of the past year's work.

The first thing on the program was a review and inspection of the entire scout body by Captain Chalmers, who had unexpectedly obtained leave of absence for the occasion. When this was over, there followed a brief pause, during which the captain, standing before the long, double row of boyish figures, in their trim, immaculate uniforms, conferred in whispers with Scoutmaster Curtis, whom he had summoned from the line. Instantly a faint, scarcely perceptible stir swept down the lines of waiting scouts. What was coming? they asked themselves eagerly. Dale Tompkins caught the captain's glance fixed on him for a moment, and wondered uneasily whether anything was the matter with his equipment. He had no time to grow seriously disturbed, however, before Mr. Curtis returned to the head of the troop and the captain faced the audience.

"I dare say you have all heard more or less about our scout law and the high principles it inculcates in every boy who promises to obey it," he said in his pleasant, easy manner. "I'd like to tell you briefly about the way two scouts right here in our own town applied some of the most vital of these principles. The first incident happened late last fall, when a powerfully charged electric wire was blown down in a storm and dangled in the street. A small boy saw it, and, without realizing the danger, grasped it in both hands. Instantly the current, passing into his body, made him helpless. He screamed with pain and struggled to tear himself loose, but in the throng that quickly gathered no one dared to touch him. No one, that is, until one of the scouts I speak of appeared. He had been a tenderfoot only a few days, but he was a true scout at heart. Without hesitation he gripped the child by one shoulder and was instantly flung the width of the street. Recovering, he remembered something he had read about electricity and insulation, remembered that paper was a good non-conductor and rubber even better. In a flash he had wrapped about his hands some of the newspapers he carried, flung down his waterproof delivery-bag to stand on, and went again to the aid of the child, this time successfully. It was not only a brave deed, but he kept his head; and when the danger was over he slipped quietly away without waiting for either praise or thanks."

A burst of applause and hand-clapping came from the audience, and while waiting for it to subside the captain glanced again toward Dale Tompkins. This time he did not meet the boy's questioning glance, but saw only drooping lids and a face flushed crimson. His smile deepened a little as he raised one hand for silence.

"A few months later the other scout was skating with a companion on Crystal Lake. He could swim only a few strokes, but when the second boy broke through the ice he did not hesitate an instant in going to his rescue. He was dragged into the water and nearly drowned, but he, too, kept his head and held up his friend until help came.

"I like to think that the actions of those two boys was typical rather than exceptional. I don't believe there is a scout here," his glance swept the line of khaki-clad figures for an instant, "who, given the chance to risk his life for another, would not respond exactly as these boys did. When I heard of what they had done I applied to our national council for honor medals such as are awarded to scouts for the saving of life. They arrived some time ago, but I awaited this occasion to present them. Scouts Dale Tompkins and Frank Sanson will please step forward."

Amid the thunder of applause that followed, Captain Chalmers turned and faced the line of scouts again, two small square boxes in his hand. Dazed, bewildered, and blushing furiously, Dale stood as if rooted to the spot until Harry Vedder gave him a sharp dig in the ribs. Then he stumbled forward a few steps, realized that another halting figure was beside him, and, recovering a little, but with face still flushing, he crossed the interminable space to where the captain stood.

One thing only was he thankful for at that moment–the heartening touch of Sanson's shoulder against his own. To have faced the ordeal alone would have been almost intolerable. He did not raise his eyes above the third button on the captain's coat, and so he missed the look of pride and approval the man bent on him as he pinned the silver cross upon the boy's left breast.

"It is a great pleasure for me to give you this," he said, "and to thank you in the name of the national council for having proved so great a credit to the scouts."

Dale's hand went up, and he saluted. "Thank you, sir," he said in a low tone.

"And remember, both of you," went on the captain, when he had placed the second cross on Sanson's coat, "that it isn't the medal that counts, but the deed which has earned it."

As the boys turned and marched back to their places the applause burst out again with renewed vigor until it seemed as if it would never cease. But at length it died away and the entertainment proceeded. Troop Three started off with an exhibition of signaling which was swift, snappy, and on the minute. Then came some tent-erecting, and, following that, two troops combined to give an elaborate and graphic exhibition of their expertness in first aid, which met with much favor. When this was over, the troops who had finished lined up and stood at ease on either side of the center to give Troop Five room for their evolutions.

Bob Gibson's position was directly in front of the closed double doors leading into the hall. He had scarcely taken it before he became conscious of a distinct odor of something burning. For a moment he was uneasy; then he remembered that there was a register just behind him, and decided that the janitor had probably chosen this auspicious moment to consume in the furnace the rubbishy accumulation of several offices on the lower floors.

When the applause that greeted their appearance had subsided, Mr. Curtis stepped forward to explain briefly the purpose of their drill. He had scarcely spoken more than a sentence or two when Gibson became aware of a slight stir among some of the audience and noticed that a number of those in the front row seemed to be staring fixedly at his feet.

A flush mounted to Bob's forehead. He was quite sure his shoes were immaculately polished. He also realized perfectly that he ought not notice the audience, but remain rigidly at attention. But presently curiosity got the better of discipline. He shot a furtive glance at his feet–a glance that flashed sidewise beyond the trim shoes and well-fitting leggings to rest in dumb, horrified amazement on the crack extending below the double doors, through which a thin line of smoke was slowly trickling.

CHAPTER XXXI

THE RIOT WEDGE

For a long moment Bob Gibson stood like one petrified. He thought of the crowd, of the narrow, twisted stairs, of panic. What ought he do? What was there possible for him to do? He tried to remember what the scout book said about fires and panics, but his brain seemed numb. Before it had cleared there came a choking cry from the other side, and Bennie Rhead, the youngest scout in the troop, slipped out of the line, and before any one could stop him, had jerked open the door to let in a rolling cloud of dense black smoke.

Like a flash Wesley Becker leaped after him, dragged him back, and slammed the door; but the damage was done. There was a long, gasping, concerted sigh, as of hundreds of people catching their breath in unison; in a second more the hall resounded with that cry which chills the blood and sends shivers chasing down the spine. To Gibson, standing pale and frightened, it seemed as if that whole close-packed assemblage surged up like some awful monster and rushed toward him, a bedlam of shrill sound; while out of doors the wild clamor of the fire-alarm suddenly burst forth to add horror to the scene.

Shaking and terrified, Bob nevertheless stood motionless, partly because he did not know what else to do, but mainly because the fellows on either side of him had not stirred. He dug his teeth into his under lip to keep back a frightened whimper, and then of a sudden the clear, high voice of Mr. Curtis rang out above the deafening din and turmoil:

"Troop Five prepare to form double riot wedge! One!"

Instinctively Bob leaped two paces forward and a little to the right. In like fashion the others darted to their positions with the swift precision of machines. Not a scout failed. Even Bennie Rhead, frightened as he was, made no mistake, and in a trice the wedge was complete.

"Two!" shouted the scoutmaster.

Down swung the staves, interlocking in a double barrier of stout hickory backed by equally sturdy muscle. The scoutmaster had barely time to place himself at the apex of the wedge before the mob struck it.

"Hold fast, boys!" he cried. "Brace your feet and don't let them break the line!" He flung up both arms in the faces of the maddened throng. "Stop!" he shouted. "You can't get out this way. The stairs are impassable. Stop crowding! There's no danger if you keep your heads. The fire-escapes are in good order. The windows–"

The rest was choked off by the crushing weight of the mob dashing against the barrier. Even in the second row Bob felt the double line shake and give under the strain, and instinctively he dropped a shoulder against the pressure and spread out his legs to brace himself. MacIlvaine noticed what he was doing, and shouted to the others to follow Bob's example; and presently the line steadied and held. Then a shrill whistle cut through the clamor, stilling it a little and making it possible to hear the stentorian voice of Captain Chalmers from somewhere in the rear of the crowd.

"You can't get out by the stairs! There are fire-escapes at both front and rear. Ladders will soon be raised to the other windows. There's no danger if you only keep your heads. Stop crowding and form in line at the windows. Scouts will see that these lines are kept and that the women and children are taken out first."

"Hold fast, boys!" he cried. "Brace your feet and don't let them break the line!"

An inarticulate murmur followed his words, but the wild din of a moment before was not resumed. In a moment, too, the pressure of bodies against the double line of scouts about the door began to relax as those in the rear made haste to seek other ways of escape. Presently it had ceased entirely, and as the boys straightened up from their cramped positions Mr. Curtis turned to face them.

"I'm proud of you, fellows," he said in a low, quick tone. "That was corking! Steady, now, for a minute or two longer."

That minute or two seemed the longest space of time Bob Gibson had ever known. Now that the stress and strain of strenuous action was removed he had time to think, to wonder–to be afraid. His mother and father were both here; so was Ted and little Flossie. Had they been in that awful crush? he wondered, as his anxious gaze flashed from one to another of the scurrying groups. Had they been hurt? The smoke was pouring more thickly into the hall, stinging his eyes and catching his throat in a choking sort of grip. Through the open windows came the clash and clang of engines, the muffled roar of excited crowds gathering below. Bob could see nothing of his mother or the children, and a dry sob came from his tight lips.

"'Tention!" called the scoutmaster, sharply. "We'll take the two windows at this side of the front, fellows. Line up on either side of them, and keep the crowd in order. Women and children first, remember. Left face! March!"

Bob pivoted mechanically and moved forward in step with MacIlvaine. Through the swirling smoke he could see that the other troops had gathered at different windows and were keeping the crowd in line, helping the women and small children through to the fire-escapes or out to the ladders which had just been raised. By this time the men, for the most part, had recovered from their panic and were helping in the work. Suddenly the boy caught sight of his mother in the line of people close by the next window. She was carrying Flossie, and his father had Ted over one shoulder. They both looked so calm and brave that Bob's spine stiffened, and when he caught his mother's eye a moment later he was able to smile and wave his hand almost as carelessly as if his heart wasn't pounding unevenly at the sudden realization that not a scout could stir until every one else was out of the building.

It wasn't a conscious longing for any one else's place. It was blind fear, pure and simple; and though he tried to crush it down by thinking of the people he was helping, it persisted and grew stronger, just as the smoke grew steadily denser and more choking, and the crackle of flames seemed to come from behind the closed doors with ominous distinctness. When the electric lights suddenly went out leaving only the two oil side-lamps burning dimly, it was all he could do to keep from crying out with terror. Indeed, he instinctively took a quick step out of line toward the window, but Mr. Curtis's cool voice halted him:

"Steady, Bob. Not quite yet."

The boy's fingers dug into his palms and he stepped quickly back into his place, a flush of shame mantling his cheeks. Had any of the other fellows noticed? he wondered. His questioning glance swept along the line and was suddenly arrested by the face of Dale Tompkins, who stood a little beyond.

Dale was not looking at him; on the contrary, he was staring back into the murky gloom of the big room with an expression of such desperate anxiety and fear that Gibson's heart leaped, and instinctively he turned his head to see what new peril threatened. When he glanced back, after a scrutiny that revealed nothing unexpected, Tompkins had disappeared.

"He's gone!" gasped the boy, his surprise mingled with a touch of envy. "He's cut out and got away!"

But Dale had not run away. At that very moment, instead of flying panic-stricken to a window, as Bob supposed, he was groping his way through the darkness toward the farther end of the smoke-filled hall. As he passed behind the line of scouts and pushed on through the thinning throng of frightened people, fear filled his soul and brought a tortured look into his smarting eyes—that fear for another which is often so much more gripping than the fear for self.

Ages ago, it seemed to the anxious boy, Ranny Phelps had disappeared in this same direction and had not returned. Dale had caught a disjointed word or two about water-buckets, but where they were or to what use Ranny meant to put them he did not know. With growing alarm he had watched and waited, and then, unable to stand the suspense another instant, he slipped out of the line and went to seek his friend.

As he passed the double doors the smoke seemed to thicken, causing him to choke and sputter. Where was it coming from, he wondered dazedly. It was as if great volumes were pouring freely into the hall, yet the doors to the corridor had been closed from the first.

He stumbled over a chair and nearly fell. Recovering, his outstretched hands struck the wall, and he began to feel his way along it. Presently his fingers gripped the edge of a door-casing, and he staggered back as a fresh burst of suffocating fumes caught his lungs with a smothering clutch.

For an instant he stood there reeling. Then in a flash he remembered the coat-room, remembered the narrow pair of stairs leading down from one corner with a row of red fire-buckets on a bench beside it. These were the buckets Ranny had come for. The door to the stairs was—open!

He caught his breath with a dry sob and plunged into the pitchy darkness of the smaller room. Two steps he took—three. Then his foot struck against something, and he fell forward over a body stretched out on the floor, his out-thrust arms reaching beyond it.

For a moment he thought it was all over. His senses were swimming in the clouds of deadly smoke pouring up from below, and it took an appreciable second or two to realize that the thing one hand clutched instinctively was the edge of an open door. Almost as instinctively he summoned all his strength and flung it to. The resulting slam came as something indistinct and far away. He wondered if he were losing consciousness, and in the same breath his jaw squared with the stubborn determination that he would not–he must not! As he reached up to tear the wide handkerchief from about his neck his fingers brushed the silver cross pinned to his left breast, and the touch seemed to give him fresh courage.

With feverish haste he felt for Ranny's wrists, knotted the neckerchief about them, and, drawing them over his head, began to crawl toward the door. Too late he remembered the water in the buckets and wished he had thought to dip a handkerchief in that to breathe through. Doubtless it was that very idea which had brought Ranny himself here. But he did not dare turn back, and after all, now that the stair door was closed, the smoke did not seem quite so dense, especially down here on the floor.

He reached the door and crawled through, dragging his helpless burden with him. Through the smoke the farther windows were vaguely outlined against a flickering, reddish background. A brighter line of fire marked the crack beneath the double doors. Under his body, too, the floor felt hot, and he could sense a queer, uneven pulsation as if the boards were moving. What if the flames should burst through before they could get away? What if–

"Dale! Ranny! Where are you?"

It was the scoutmaster's voice, and Dale's broke a little as he answered. In another moment Mr. Curtis was beside him, bending to lift the unconscious boy in his arms.

"Are you all right?" he asked tersely as he turned toward the windows.

"Yes."

Scrambling to his feet, Dale stumbled after him. A crackling roar from behind the closed doors made him shiver. The windows were clear. Every one seemed to have left the hall save a single figure standing beside the nearest opening, one leg already over the sill.

"Quick, Wes!" snapped Mr. Curtis. "Get out on the ladder and take him. Fireman's lift, you know."

Becker obeyed swiftly, and, swinging the limp body over his shoulder, disappeared from view.

"Now, Dale," ordered the scoutmaster. "You–"

The words were drowned in a crashing roar as the doors fell in. There was a sudden, blinding burst of flame, a wave of scorching heat that seemed to sear into Dale's very soul. He flung up both hands before his eyes, and, as he did so, two arms grasped him about the body and fairly whirled him through the window to the ladder.

"Catch hold and slide!" commanded the scoutmaster. "Hustle!"

Mechanically, as he had done a score of times in their fire-drills from the roof of Mr. Curtis' barn, Dale curled arms and legs about the ladder sides, shut his eyes, and slid. Part way down a blast of heat struck his face; then hands caught him, easing the descent, and he found himself on the ground, with firemen all around and the cool spray from one of the big, brass-nozzled hoses drifting across him. He had scarcely time to step away from the ladder when Mr. Curtis, with hair singed and clothes smoking, shot out of the flame-tinged smoke and came down with a rush, while from the anxious crowd there burst a loud cheer of relief and laxing tension.

Dale blinked and drew the clean air into his lungs with long, uneven breaths. Then the grimy face of Court Parker popped up suddenly before him.

"Where's Wes, and–and Ranny?" demanded Tompkins sharply.

"Over there."

Dale pushed his way across the street and up to the edge of a circle that some of the scouts had formed about a small group on the farther sidewalk. This opened to let him through, and as he stood looking down on the handsome, blackened, pallid face of the boy Becker and MacIlvaine were working over, something seemed to grip his throat and squeeze it tight.

"Is he–" he stammered, "will he–"

Becker glanced up and nodded reassuringly. "He's coming round all right. He's pretty well done up, that's all."

Under the shadowy tangle of disordered hair Ranny's lids suddenly lifted, and the blue eyes looked straight up into Dale's face. For a second there was absolutely no expression in them. Then something flickered into the glance that made Dale's heart leap and sent the blood tingling to the roots of his hair. A moment later the pale lips moved, and he bent swiftly to catch the words.

"I knew–you'd come–chum," Ranny whispered. Then his lips curved in a rueful smile. "Of all the rotten luck!" he murmured. "They never saw–our drill."